Travelling Collection

BRANCH LOCATED AT

Love is
a time of enchantment:
in it all days are fair and all fields
green. Youth is blest by it,
old age made benign:
the eyes of love see
roses blooming in December,
and sunshine through rain. Verily
is the time of true-love
a time of enchantment — and
Oh! how eager is woman
to be bewitched!

JACOBITE SUMMER

When Bonny Prince Charlie fled
Scotland after the destruction of
his army at Culloden, he vowed to
return. Five years later he spent ten
days in London, although his reason
for doing so is a mystery. How Anna
becomes involved with the Jacobite
and Hanoverian secret services and
finds ' herself the unwilling pawn of
two equally attractive but ruthless
men, and how for one moment, in
that summer of 1750, the fate of
England is in her hands, is told
in this possible explanation for the
Prince's mysterious visit.

CLARE ROSSITER

◆

JACOBITE SUMMER

Complete and Unabridged

ULVERSCROFT
Leicester

First published in Great Britain

First Large Print Edition
published 1996

British Library CIP Data

Rossiter, Clare
Jacobite summer.—Large print ed.—
Ulverscroft large print series: romance
I. Title
823.914 [F]

ISBN 0–7089–3452–8

Published by
F. A. Thorpe (Publishing) Ltd.
Anstey, Leicestershire
Set by Words & Graphics Ltd.
Anstey, Leicestershire
Printed and bound in Great Britain by
T. J. Press (Padstow) Ltd., Padstow, Cornwall

This book is printed on acid-free paper

1

"DON'T go!"

As soon as she had spoken Anna bent her head and wished she had stayed silent.

The young man's hands grew still as he viewed her reflection through the mirror over the mantelpiece, before continuing to flick imaginary dust from his yellow satin coat, he smiled slightly and lifted his eyebrows in query.

"Whyever not, Sis?" he asked easily, arranging the snowy folds of his lace cravat with one finger.

"Kit — you know why not!" Anna protested.

"Indeed I do not, dearest sister."

She knew from the tone of his voice that he was irritated and yet felt herself constrained to continue.

"You — will l–lose," she said wretchedly. "You always do."

"Not so," said her brother, making a show of admiring the small black patch placed carefully beside his mouth. "Not so, sweet sister. I have won several times this month and doubtless will do so again — in fact I feel that Lady Luck will be with me tonight, so have no fear with regard to our precious stock of guineas."

He blew a kiss to her reflection before, turning, he made an elaborate bow and swept from the room, his red heels tapping on the wooden floor.

Anna sighed as she heard him leave the house and after a moment picked up her embroidery again, only to let the material lie crumpled in her lap and the needle hang lax between her fingers as she gazed blankly at the gaily coloured silks, her mind far away from the small parlour and the noises of London.

Less than a year ago they had been secure in a small country town, her father the respected, scholarly Vicar. Only when he died had they discovered how far removed from the cares and worries of everyday life he had been; with him had died his stipend and the only thing he had to leave his children besides a collection of books, were several longstanding and

2

unpaid debts. The books were sold to cover these and with the little left Anna and Christopher came to London in the hopes of making their living.

Anna knew now that it had been a mistake to leave Alstead and their acquaintances, but at the time it had seemed sensible to settle in the City and offer their talents as teachers to the younger inhabitants of the Capital. The prospect of a small school had not seemed beyond the bounds of possibility to their naïve and innocent minds, but now, with the memory of the pile of bills clustering in the drawer of the small bureau behind her, Anna could only smile sadly at the thought of how foolish they had been.

Slowly, she raised her head and glanced round the shabby room, her eyes lingering on the empty places where the few treasures they had brought with them, had once stood. Now there was nothing left to sell. She had managed to placate the Landlady for a few more days, but by the end of the week she would again be demanding the rent for the rooms they occupied.

'And yet,' she thought mutinously, as she stabbed her needle into the material. 'And yet we would have managed, but for one thing . . . '

In coming to London and making new friends her brother had discovered something quite unexpected. As children their father had often regaled them with tales of how his own father had lost his wealth through an uncontrollable urge to gamble and now that urge had reasserted itself in his grandson.

Once introduced to cards by his erstwhile friends, no other thought had filled Kit's mind. He spent every possible moment at the gaming tables, convinced, despite his losses that he had only to play another game to win. And in all this he was encouraged by one man, a Captain Rafe Bellamy, late of the army, who urged him on to greater excesses with such verve and enthusiasm that soon Anna viewed the ex-soldier with unquenchable dislike, convinced that the older man was solely responsible for her brother's lapse.

Someone knocking on the front door brought the girl out of her reverie and she sat forward, listening to the voices below in the forlorn hope that her brother had relented and returned. Not recognising the voice, she relaxed and had just taken up her sewing again when after a discreet tap the small maid of the house opened the door and poked her head into the room.

"A Captain Bellamy, miss," she announced.

Anna's lips tightened. "Thank you, Betsy," she said. "Pray tell Captain Bellamy that my brother is out."

A few minutes later the maid returned, breathing heavily after her second ascent of the long and steep stairs. "Captain Bellamy's compliments, miss," she panted, "but his business is with you."

Anna stared blankly at her, until conscious of the speculation in the other's gaze, she forced herself to smile and say easily,

"Why to be sure, the Captain is lending me a book belonging to his sister. I had forgot. Be so good as to show him up, Betsy."

When the man entered, Anna was standing beside the window, apparently intent upon the scene below. For a moment she appeared unaware of his entrance and a faint smile gleamed in the depths of his grey eyes as he closed the door behind him with an audible snap.

"Your servant, Miss Stanton," he said, coming forward and Anna was forced to acknowledge his presence, dropping a brief curtsey but making no pretence of pleasure at his company.

"I am sure you are wondering at my presence here," he began easily, "but as my explanation may take some while, can we not be seated?"

Wondering at his cool assumption, Anna gestured him to a chair by the fireplace and seated herself on the deep windowsill. Flicking apart the skirts of his lilac satin coat with the dexterity of long practice, he sat down, one hand on the hilt of his sword, making no effort to hide his calm scrutiny.

Anna's eyebrows rose under his cool gaze and she made a quickly stifled gesture of impatience before she spoke. "Pray still my curiosity, sir," she said. "My time is limited and I have much to do."

"Of course," he agreed, glancing round

the empty room devoid of books or means of making music and she knew that he was aware how empty her evenings were.

"Only hear me out and I shall leave you to your — business." He leaned his broad shoulders back against the chair, making the elderly piece of furniture creak alarmingly and toyed with the silver tassel attached to his sword. "Forgive me asking, Miss Stanton, but is Kit at the gaming tables?"

Anna drew a quick breath. "You know he is," she said sharply.

The gentleman smiled lazily. "I do not *know*," he corrected her, "not having seen him this evening — but I believe that he is at his club."

"To which you introduced him," Anna burst out.

Thin dark eyebrows rose. "If not I, then someone else. You may be sure he was ripe for plucking!"

Her eyes growing wide as a suspicion struck her, Anna jumped to her feet. "Are you a c-cardsharp?" she demanded.

Captain Bellamy laughed shortly. "Not I," he said, amused. "You may be sure that your brother is safe from any such person. Not even the least self-respecting cardsharp would be interested in such poor pickings as Kit Stanton's pockets."

Slowly Anna sat down, her eyes still on the figure in the chair opposite. "I believe you introduced him to those gambling dens deliberately," she said.

A thin smile flickered across the face of the man watching her. "I thought you were more astute than your brother," he commented.

"B-but why?" the girl asked, bewildered.

Instead of answering her, the soldier stood up and crossed to a table by the wall. "Will you allow me to pour some wine?" he asked and without waiting for her assent, filled two glasses, handing one to her before he reseated himself.

The room had grown dim, the shadows of the spring evening filling the corners with darkness. Anna rose to her feet and taking a taper held it to the coals in the fireplace and lit the candles on the table by her guest's elbow, before lighting those on the mantelpiece. After the dimness the room sprang into prominence and she did as her brother had done and

8

examined through the mirror the figure in the chair behind her.

As though aware of her gaze Captain Bellamy looked up and catching her eyes raised his glass to her in silent toast. Flushing, Anna turned hurriedly away and would have returned to her seat in the window but his voice stopped her as she crossed the room.

"Miss Stanton — You make it clear that you have little wish for my company, but what I have to say is of importance and something I would not have bandied about between your landlady and her servants."

As he spoke he rose and crossed the room swiftly and silently to open the door and step out onto the landing. Still silently, he looked up and down the dark well of the stairs, listening for a moment before he came back into the room, closing the door behind him.

"I vow you would do well at Drury Lane," commented the girl, letting her amusement show, but ignoring this sally, he gestured to the chair opposite the one he had vacated.

"Sit down, Miss Stanton and not so far from me, if you please. I would prefer not to shout."

Anna lifted her chin at his peremptory tone, but did as she was bidden, realising that she must hear him out if her growing curiosity was to be satisfied.

"Well, sir?" she asked, settling her skirts and folding her hands neatly in her lap, but now her guest seemed to find conversation difficult and took a swift turn about the room, before seating himself on the other side of the meagre fire, he took up his glass again, turning it round between his long fingers, while he watched the deep red liquid, glowing in the candlelight.

"The weather has been very warm of late, has it not?" said Anna politely, "'though, perhaps a little cool for the time of year."

The glass was abruptly still. "I did not come here to discuss the weather — "

"Forgive me, I thought you needed a little time to collect your thoughts. Perhaps, if you are going to be very long in doing so, you would be so kind as to give me my embroidery. It's just

10

beside you on the table."

He dropped the linen into her lap and watched as she composedly snipped a length of silk and threaded a needle, only a slight tremor of her hands betraying her feelings to his intent gaze.

"Your mother was Lydia Grey before she married and I believe that at one time she was governess to a Miss Drelincourt."

Anna stared at him in amazement, her needle poised to take a stitch. "That is so — but h-how did you know?"

"I made it my business to find out," Captain Bellamy told her baldly.

"But — why? What possible reason can you have?"

"A very good one, as you shall presently understand. And your brother, the esteemed Kit, wishes to join the army?"

"He must have told you so."

"Many times," was the curt, almost impatient reply and she looked at him silently, wondering where this strange conversation could possibly lead.

"I also know how deeply in debt you both are — "

"That, sir, is our business and I would

have thought that as a gentleman you would have had the courtesy not to mention it."

He smiled at the vehemence in her voice. "It's well known," he told her lazily. "Kit makes no secret of the matter."

Anna hung her head. "Then he should have more sensibility."

The soldier reached into a pocket. "I imagine you have a drawerful of these tucked away somewhere," he said quietly and laid the sheaf of papers on Anna's knee.

Eyes wide, she stared into his impassive face before turning her gaze to the crumpled papers in her lap. Almost reluctantly she examined them, some premonition of disaster making her hands slow to move. Incredulity and then anguish crossed her face.

"Oh, dear God!" she whispered, her trembling hands falling to cover the bills, lying on the worn material of her gown. "So much!" Quickly she thumbed through the papers, taking in an amount here, a name there. "And most owed to you."

"I am afraid so — the others I have bought up."

"But — why?" The question was almost a cry, as she put up a hand to cover her mouth.

His glance was impersonal as he watched her distress. "I'll explain later," he said quietly, "but first I want to be sure that you are aware of the possible consequences of your brother's indiscretions." He finished his wine and set the glass down on the table at his elbow. "Those scribbled notes of his amount to something over two thousand guineas. I believe I am right in suspecting that he could not make repayment?" He looked at her enquiringly.

"We could not repay it, were it two hundred pounds," the girl was forced to admit.

"Were I to demand payment, I could have him committed to a debtor's prison and all his goods seized."

"Why have you ruined us?" Anna demanded, bitterly. "You must have made him — influenced him into gaming with you — " In her agitation she gripped the needlework in her lap, crushing it

13

between her hands, only becoming aware of the sharp point folded into the linen, when the thin needle ran into her palm and snapped in half.

Anna stared at the broken end protruding from her hand and feeling a little sick was making an ineffectual attempt to remove it, when her hand was taken and carried nearer the light. Almost before she was aware of the soldier's intention, strong fingers had pulled the sliver of steel free and tossed it into the fire. A lace handkerchief was dropped into her hand and Captain Bellamy returned to his seat opposite, seating himself composedly and resuming the conversation as though nothing had happened.

"And I would wager that there is half as much again owing to tradesmen," he went on, while Anna thought guiltily of fine gowns and suits, bought to match appearances with their new London friends.

Holding the handkerchief against her hand she bent her head and blinked away the tears that threatened to fall.

"However, there is a way out of your

14

difficulties. I have a proposition to make to you, Miss Stanton."

Anna looked at him warily; something telling her that they were coming to the crux of the matter. Narrowing her eyes a little, she stiffened and waited to hear what the man in front of her had to say.

"I expect you know I have left the army — what I am sure you don't know, is that I am still in His Majesty's service — but now I do his work secretly." He smiled a little at the bewilderment in her eyes. "Espionage, Miss Stanton," he explained kindly.

Anna's brow cleared. "A spy!" she exclaimed.

"Just so," Captain Bellamy acknowledged smoothly. "But, pray don't look so askance. I do assure you that I am a very respectable spy, knowing only one master and one country."

"I h-had not suspected that spying was such a noble profession," Anna told him and was pleased to note the gleam of anger that showed momentarily in his grey eyes.

"If you work for me I will buy

Kit a commission in the army, waive payment of his debts and even pay your outstanding bills for you," he said, examining his nails.

Anna stared across the fireplace at her unwelcome guest, taking in the expensive Mechlin lace at his neck and wrists as the candlelight danced on his powdered hair and satin clothes. "Work for you!" she breathed incredulously at last. "What could I do?"

"A great deal I expect. Be sure I would not have made certain of your co-operation, if I had doubts of your worth."

She spread her hands. "I don't know anyone who could be of interest to you," she said helplessly.

"Now there you are mistaken," the man said, leaning back in his chair. "You may not know the person in whom I have an interest, but your mother did and that will give you the entry."

"Miss Drelincourt!" exclaimed the girl.

"Exactly. 'Though she is married and now Lady Primrose."

"Then all this tangle has been for nothing — I've never met the lady,"

16

Anna told him positively.

"All things can be arranged," she was told with infuriating calm, but just as Captain Bellamy seemed on the point of telling her more, the bell in the street below them jangled stridently, making him break off his explanation. Reaching forward he scooped the bills from her lap, returning them to his deep pocket as her brother's voice could be heard in the hall.

"I need hardly tell you to keep this to yourself," he said quietly. "One word out of place and Kit will see the inside of a debtor's prison, you have my word on it."

Meeting his eyes, Anna shivered at the cold implacability in their depths and nodded quickly as her brother burst into the room.

"Well of all the things!" he began indignantly. "We were to meet at Lady Granger's and yet I find you here, ensconced with my sister." He glanced from one to the other, and grinned slightly. "And I had not even suspected that you had a liking for each other."

"Why should you know everything?" asked the soldier softly, taking up his hat and settling the sword at his side. "Miss Anna and I have spent a very . . . interesting time together. The first of many, I trust."

Taking the younger man's arm, he swept Anna an elaborate bow, holding her glance meaningly for a second, before ushering the other out of the room.

Held almost spellbound until she heard the heavy front door close behind them, Anna crossed to the window and watched as they walked along the street, her brother seeming short and slim beside the soldier's height and presence. Sinking down onto the windowseat, she touched the smear of blood on her hand wondering if she could have dreamed the events of the past hour.

Sleep that night was almost impossible and she dozed fitfully, until her brother came home in the small hours. Soon a grey light began to creep into her room and she dragged a shawl round her shoulders and read a book until the household was astir.

Kit seemed in an unusually exuberant

mood as he joined her for breakfast, dropping a heavy purse into her lap as he passed. "You see, I don't always lose," he told her triumphantly, as she loosened the string and peered inside. "There's enough there to settle the worst of the bills — and some over for tonight's play."

"Where did you get it?" she asked, already knowing the answer.

"I won it at cards, dear sister," he said, cutting a slice from the joint of beef beside his plate. "Take my advice and use some of it to sweeten our Lady Landlord. It might improve her choice of butcher."

"Who did you win it from?" Anna asked, not looking at him.

"Rafe Bellamy — I've never known him play so badly."

Anna's hands closed over the purse, a prick of pain reminding her of the wound she had sustained the night before.

"I — th-thought you owed him money," she said tonelessly.

Her brother shrugged. "He said he'd wait," he told her carelessly.

"You owe him money, Kit. You should

19

not have taken it."

He turned his head to stare at her. "Don't fly into a rage with me. He wouldn't take it. He said it would spoil my run of luck."

"Your run of luck!" she flung at him angrily. "Don't you realise what you have done? Does all that our Father taught you mean nothing? Don't you care about our family honour and pride any more?"

"I've done nothing that a gentleman need be ashamed of," he muttered sullenly. "You take too much upon yourself sister Anna, when you think to chastise me."

He glowered at her, looking so much like a sulky small boy that against her will her mood was softened and she found herself smiling at him.

"I wish you wouldn't gamble," she said, mildly, wishing that there was a father's hand to guide him.

"Now don't you see, Sis, that I can't stop. Rafe says that I must keep playing if I hope to recoup my losses."

Anna stared at him in perplexity, knowing that such logic was not sound, but only too well aware that she could never convince her brother of the fact.

"Have you any pupils coming today?" he asked a little later, with an attempt to change the subject.

"What? Oh, no," answered his sister, waking from the deep reverie that held her. "My last two have gone away to school."

"You must look for some more," Kit advised. "Place an advertisement in the paper."

"Perhaps," Anna agreed mechanically, knowing that she was too much occupied with thoughts of the previous evening's events to give her mind to any more mundane happening.

"Are you seeing Captain Bellamy today?" she asked, staring out of the window.

"Not until this evening — why? Not sweet on him are you, Anna?"

"No, of course not," she answered quickly. "I — I wondered, that's all."

"Because if you are," he went on pursuing the subject relentlessly, "I wouldn't countenance it at all. You'd find yourself in Queer Street, if you gave your heart to him, I can tell you.

21

Love 'em and leave 'em is Rafe Bellamy's motto."

"Are you trying to tell me that Captain Bellamy is a rake?" she enquired with interest.

"Really Anna, where do you acquire your language?" asked Kit, mortified. "Nothing of the sort, I do assure you, wouldn't let the fellow meet with you if he was, but he likes — *light* ladies, if you take my meaning." He paused and looked at his sister enquiringly. "*What* did you say he was doing here last night?"

"I don't think I did, but I believe he came to meet you."

"He was talking about the army, Sis. You'd never believe the adventures he had . . . he did just drop a hint that he might consider buying me a commission."

Anna looked up and reading the hope in Kit's eyes, smiled slightly. "You mustn't put too much hope on it," she said. "Why should he do such a thing?"

Her brother shrugged. "Friendship, I suppose. He said it all depended upon the outcome of some negotiations he was undertaking."

Silence fell with his words and Anna sat down abruptly, biting her lip as she recalled only too well the other possibility presented to her by the soldier.

"I think I'll take a turn around the square," said her brother from the window. "Will you come, the day's warm for early May?"

She shook her head hurriedly. "N-no. I have a headache," she excused herself, but although she waited in all day there was no sign of her expected visitor.

By the next afternoon her nerves were at full stretch and when the front door bell made its impatient summons, she started to her feet, dropping her needlework, even before she heard the familiar voice in the hall.

"My dear Miss Stanton," exclaimed Captain Bellamy entering without waiting to be announced. "I appear to have startled you."

Retrieving her embroidery, he led her to a chair and waited while she regained her composure.

"Kit is with a friend, admiring some

newly acquired horse-flesh. I can assure you that he will be some time." He paused and watched her downcast head for a few minutes. "I take it that you have an answer to the proposition I made the other night."

Raising her eyes she searched his face, realising that he had deliberately refrained from calling on her before in the knowledge that the delay would make her assent more certain. "I have no choice have I?" she said.

"None." Reaching across he removed the crumpled linen from her nervous fingers and dropped it on the table. "Between blood and creases, miss, it will hardly be worth a stitch soon," he remarked.

"What do you want me to do?"

"Nothing too arduous. I wish you to gain entry to Lady Primrose's house in Essex Street."

"To be invited there, you mean?" she asked doubtfully.

"More than that. I want you to live there."

"L-Live there!" The slight stutter that came when she was nervous or surprised was much in evidence. "B-but *how*?"

With one arm on the mantelpiece, he looked down at her. "Lady Primrose is much taken up at the moment by the arrival of her niece and nephew from Ireland. The niece in particular, I am informed is proving more than a little difficult to manage. I have arranged that you shall do her a little service — I am sure that you will be able to inveigle yourself into accompanying the young lady home and once there I shall rely on you to remind Lady Primrose of your mother's acquaintanceship . . . after which it should be easy to come by an invitation to stay or even an offer of employment."

Silence fell in the quiet room, the sounds of the distant traffic carrying to the girl's ears. As though compelled she glanced up and met his gaze. A shaft of thin spring sunlight crossed the room and touched the man before her, highlighting the green velvet coat and striking unlikely fire from his hair. Under the thin covering of powder Anna realised for the first time that Captain Bellamy's hair was a deep shade of red.

"Whatever happens you must insert yourself into a position of trust in that household — "

"I cannot!" Anna surprised herself by saying flatly. "What you ask is impossible. You want me to make friends with them and then — to betray them."

"Remember Kit."

She closed her eyes at the cool words.

"Once in the debtor's prison, he'll never get out. Can you imagine him shut in a filthy, dark cell all day? I assure you he wouldn't thank you for your morals, Miss Stanton. And have you considered what would happen to yourself? Kit tells me you have no relations to help — how long would it be I wonder before you were turned from this house to fend for yourself among the dregs of the town?"

"I'd manage," she said, stubbornly.

"I doubt it . . . And Kit, would *he* manage? I even wonder how long he'd survive, in the filth and dirt, before a prison fever carried him off."

Anna shuddered and looked away. "What have I to do?" she asked tonelessly, her brief mutiny over for the moment.

Seating himself opposite, he leaned forward. "I have it upon the best authority that Miss Drelincourt will go shopping in the Strand tomorrow afternoon. There you will take yourself also," he paused and ran his eye over her blue silk gown before he continued, "dressed, I may say, not as you are now, but in a manner suited to a poor, but genteel person. Have you such a gown?"

Reviewing her meagre wardrobe, Anna recalled the plain lavender gown in which she had arrived in London and nodded.

"Be outside Masham's the milliners at three of the clock and hold yourself in readiness to perform some service for Miss Drelincourt."

"H-how shall I know her?"

He smiled wryly. "I hope she will prove the only lady in need of your services. However she is a little taller than you, with a profusion of blonde ringlets, a liking for large panniers to her petticoats and a taste for elaborate hats." Seeing Anna's startled expression

Captain Bellamy felt called up to explain. "She is a very young lady and not long left her native Ireland."

"How fortunate for me," remarked Anna drily.

A gleam of real amusement appeared in the soldier's eyes but was quickly hidden as he bent to collect his hat and prepared to take his leave.

"One moment, sir."

Anna's cool voice hung in the air and he turned to look at her enquiringly.

"My brother, Captain Bellamy. You promised Kit a commission."

"We shall go to the War Office this afternoon," he assured her easily. "By this evening he shall be in His Majesty's service." He swept her a neat bow and placed his hand on the door handle, but again she spoke.

"Captain Bellamy."

"Marm?" Slight impatience sounded in his voice as he waited for her question.

"Why do I have to spy on the Primroses? May I ask who they are to have incurred your interest?"

For a moment he stared at her, one hand poised on the handle of the door.

"Have you never heard of Jacobites, Miss Stanton?" he asked softly and while she was still taking in the possibilities of his words, the door closed quietly behind him.

2

ANNA dressed with extra care the next afternoon and then, as she had come to know the thoroughfares of London quite well during the last few months, walked quickly to the Strand, surprised by the number of people crowding the streets. No-one took any notice of her and she knew that in her sombre gown and cloak with her neat chip-straw hat, she looked like a merchant's respectable daughter.

A church clock pealed the quarter to the hour and she hurried on, hastening her tread to be in time for the arranged meeting. Since the previous evening she had given much thought as to how the introduction might be arranged and had thought of many wild and unlikely schemes, but not even her wildest imaginings had prepared her for the eventuality when it happened.

She had read Mrs Masham's hanging sign from afar and had slowed her pace a little, wondering whether to wait near the shop or not, when a knot of fashionably dressed people came out, chattering among themselves, and Anna had no difficulty in recognising Miss Drelincourt among them; a blonde beauty with golden hair shining in the thin spring sun she put her companions in the shade as she talked vivaciously to her friends.

Suddenly a shouting, pushing gang of youths ran up the street and at the same moment a decrepit coach rounded the corner from the other direction and clattered towards the unconscious group beside the doorstep.

Anna started forward and as she did so, the gang reached the mantua-maker's. For a moment there was confusion as the gentleman tried to shield the ladies and then as the driver of the coach whipped up his broken-backed animals, Miss Drelincourt was thrust forward against the country girl.

The force sent them both blundering forward, but as Anna had been expecting something of the kind, she regained her balance quickly and pulled the other girl back to safety. As she did so a hand took her in the small of the back sending her to her knees almost under the wheels of the speeding carriage. Her hat was knocked from her head by the force of her fall and she watched in fascinated horror as the iron rim of the heavy wheel crushed the wide straw brim.

Gradually the rumble of the vehicle passed into the distance and raising her head, Anna realised that the noisy boys had vanished as quickly as they had appeared and that now the street was almost deserted except for Miss Drelincourt and the friends who milled about her and the stout form of Mrs Masham, who had heard the commotion and had come out of her shop to join in the excitement.

"Come in and sit down to recover," she was urging.

"Yes, but first I must thank this lady," answered a voice with the suspicion of an Irish brogue and Anna who was still sitting on the cobblestones looked up and found herself staring into smiling blue eyes.

"You saved my life," said their owner

dramatically "and for that I am eternally grateful."

Climbing somewhat shakily to her feet, Anna attempted to brush the city dust and dirt from her skirts and murmured a polite disclaimer as she retrieved her ill treated hat.

"Indeed it's true. You must come into the shop with me and good Mrs Masham will find us a glass of wine while we recover ourselves."

The dressmaker made haste to agree and taking Anna's arm urged her into the shop. Anna had never been in such an establishment before and her eyes opened wide at the array of materials and ribbons displayed among the elegant chairs and delicate tables.

The accident had shaken her more than she cared to admit and the wine that was offered made her head spin. Knowing that she must keep her wits about her, Anna sipped cautiously and did her best to clear her brain.

"Such behaviour!" snorted the hovering dressmaker. "It wouldn't have been allowed in my young day. I don't know what things are coming to, indeed I don't.

What *dear* Miss Drelincourt must think of our London ways — "

The girl in the blue silk gown tossed back her curls and laughed. "We have much the same thing in Ireland, I do assure you. Luckily there's no harm done."

"The other young lady's hurt," the older woman pointed out suddenly and Anna raised her eyes to find that they were all looking at her. Following their concerted gaze, she was startled to see blood upon her ruined chipstraw hat and hastily lifting her hand, found a deep cut across the palm.

"Good gracious!" she exclaimed faintly as Mrs Masham covered the welling blood with a square of linen.

"It needs attention," the older woman announced.

"She shall come home with me," pronounced Miss Drelincourt firmly. "Jason, find us two chairs, if you please and send a boy for the physician."

Within minutes Anna was being tucked into a sedan-chair and carried swiftly through the Strand to Essex Street which was nearby. Solicitous hands helped her up the stairs and into a tall imposing house. Miss Drelincourt swept her into a comfortably furnished parlour and, sinking down into a chair, Anna realised that she had achieved her goal almost without any conscious action on her own part.

"Really there is no need — I feel I am imposing," she felt constrained to say. "Nonsense," cried the Irish girl, tossing her hat and cloak onto a chair. "The doctor will be here shortly, but first let me look at your hand."

Cool fingers removed the linen and turned her hand to the light. "Mm — well. I've seen worse in the hunting field to be sure, but I'll just leave it until Dr Brown is here. Does it hurt much?"

Anna shook her head. "Hardly at all," she answered honestly.

"I'm Cecilia Drelincourt, will you tell me your name?"

"Anna Stanton. I live in Green Square with my brother — "

She stopped abruptly as a middle aged woman entered the room, her wide hoops swaying with the urgency of her movement.

"Cessy, what's this I hear of an accident?" she cried, her eyes on the girl in blue. "Are you hurt?"

"Not I, Aunt Anne, thanks to Miss Stanton here, who pulled me back from under the wheels of a coach and was hurt herself in doing so."

The older woman turned to Anna, examining her intently for a moment, before, apparently pleased with what she saw, she smiled warmly and gave the girl her hand.

"My thanks for what you did," she said simply. "Will you take a dish of tea while we await the doctor?"

Anna gratefully accepted, feeling that a cup of the innocuous brew might clear her head, which persisted in spinning in a somewhat alarming manner and leaned back with her eyes closed.

"Miss Stanton ruined her hat," she heard Miss Drelincourt say in a meaningful voice and, looking out from under her half closed eyelids, saw the two women looking at her chipstraw where it lay on the table. The younger woman touched one of the dirty white roses that Anna had pinned onto the wide brim only that morning and glanced up at her aunt. Lady Primrose touched her own lips in a gesture for silence and stole a look at Anna.

"Such a pity about your hat," she said, "it must have been very pretty."

"Yes — I am very fond of white roses. In fact I prefer them to all others," Anna said, knowing that a white rose was a Jacobite emblem and would almost certainly be accepted as proof of her own political leanings in this Jacobite household.

For a moment their eyes met and then the older woman smiled, relaxing almost perceptibly. "I do agree," she said "and one grown on an old, true bush is so much better than a new strain."

"Lady Primrose," Anna said, seizing her opportunity, "forgive my presumption, but I believe I have heard my mother speak of you?"

"Indeed, how so?"

"She was a governess before she married and often spoke of having taught you."

"What was her name?"

"Margaret Weston."

"Miss Weston! by all that's wonderful. What a coincidence to meet you like this." She sat down beside the younger woman and began to ask eager questions.

Soon she had the full story from Anna of her mother's early death and of the abortive attempt to earn a living in London.

"But what shall you do," she cried, "alone in the City when your brother leaves for the army? I own it's generous of his patron to buy his commission, but your brother should give you some consideration."

"I would not stand in his way. I shall look for some position — some employment."

Lady Primrose would have spoken, but at that moment the doctor was announced and, declaring that she could not bring herself to like blood, she departed leaving Anna to the care of her niece and the family physician.

Some time later a message having been sent to her brother, Anna found herself lying in an elegant four poster bed, with her hand bandaged and being treated with all the consideration due to an invalid. Cecilia Drelincourt had looked in before she went down to dinner and the other girl could not but admire the almond green gown though she blinked a little at the profusion of diamonds that sparkled at the Irish girl's throat and wrists.

"Sure and you look ready to sleep after your supper, but I've brought you a book of poems in case you can't close your eyes."

She bent over Anna in a cloud of perfume and dropped a small volume on the coverlet. "My brother, James, is here tonight," she confided, pausing in the doorway, her hoops swaying a little as she turned sideways to squeeze her wide skirt through the door. "You'll meet him tomorrow — I am sure that he will like you."

After she had gone Anna settled back against her pillows pondering on the shade of anxiety that had tinged the other's voice. Was her brother so formidable a character, that Cecilia Drelincourt was a little nervous of him she wondered drowsily, and fell asleep before she had decided on the answer.

Next morning she awoke with a sore hand, but no other reminder of her misadventure and when Lady Primrose sent for her, felt well enough to thank her for her care and make a tentative attempt to leave Essex Street.

The two ladies looked at each other across her head and then Lady Primrose bent forward and touched her hand.

"We had hoped that you would stay a little longer," she said.

"I cannot trespass on your hospitality any longer."

"In fact," the other went on, "Cessy and I have a proposition to put to you. My dear Miss Stanton, I gather from what you have said that you will soon have to look for a position. Forgive me for being blunt, but I understand that your situation is somewhat — difficult — at the moment."

Anna hung her head and waited for the older woman to continue.

"That being so, Cessy and I have had an idea. I am no longer young and have affairs of my own to attend to. I find that escorting Cecilia takes up time which might be spent upon more

40

important things."

Anna glanced at Miss Drelincourt to see how she was taking her aunt's plain speaking, but saw to her surprise, that by her expression she seemed to be in agreement with Lady Primrose.

"And so you see, I had just reached the conclusion that a companion would be the very thing. How fortunate, my dear, that you should appear when you did, for you are the very person for whom we are looking. Steady, sensible, of good breeding and a little older than Cessy."

"But — I hardly know how to go on in society," Anna felt forced to acknowledge, certain that the mild social functions in Alstead had hardly fitted her for London gatherings.

"Pershaw! Nothing's easier — you'll pick it up as you go along. Besides, we don't move in the forefront of society, you know. We have our own friends."

"Please do say 'yes', Miss Stanton," urged Cecilia. "I do so long to attend more functions than Aunt Anne can take me to."

Anna glanced from one to the other, feeling constrained to hesitate a little.

"W-ell," she prevaricated, "I am sure you do me a great kindness, but . . . "

"Come now, Miss Anna," said Lady Primrose, a shade impatiently and for the first time Anna caught a glimpse of the character behind the kindly, mild front and realised with a slight sense of shock that the older woman would not take kindly to having her plans thwarted, "you acknowledge, yourself, that you need a position and will have to look for a place as a governess soon. Surely it would be wise to come to us, where you will be treated as one of the family and not have to care for unruly and difficult children."

"I did not mean to give the impression that I wasn't grateful for your offer — I am afraid that I feel inadequate for the task."

"Have no fear on that score. If you're your mother's daughter you were brought up a lady," Lady Primrose said bluntly. "And I can see that she has bequeathed you her dress sense. I have no doubt that you know how to be elegant."

Anna smiled. "Then — I can only thank you for your kind offer and accept,"

42

she said and dipped into a formal curtsey, her lavender petticoats billowing.

As she rose, the door behind her opened and a young man entered, pausing at the sight of a stranger.

"Oh, James," cried Cecilia, hurrying forward to take his arm and urge him towards Anna, "this is Miss Stanton. You remember how I told you she saved me from the wheels of a coach."

"Why to be sure," said the young man, recovering from his surprise and coming forward. "Miss Stanton, I am pleased to meet you and have the opportunity of thanking you for your services to my sister."

Again Anna dropped into a curtsy as her hand was taken, glancing up as James Drelincourt carried it to his lips to find his bright blue eyes full upon her. Holding her gaze, he smiled and Anna felt her breath quicken a little at the obvious admiration in his eyes.

Murmuring a shaken disclaimer, she allowed him to lead her to a chair, sinking into the depths, while trying to hide the effect his charm was having upon her.

"Where have you been hiding?" he asked, softly, for her ears alone. "I am sure I would have heard, if you had been long in London."

"M-my brother and I live very quietly — I am afraid that I do not go about in society," she answered, hoping that her heart would cease hammering against her tight bodice.

"We must change that!" he exclaimed and turning his head called to his sister. "Cessy, Miss Stanton tells me that she does not go into society — we cannot allow such a thing."

Cecilia laughed. "Sure and nothing's easier to arrange, brother. Miss Anna has just agreed to take a position as my companion."

At once James Drelincourt's attitude changed and abandoning his relaxed appearance, he stood straighter, subjecting her to a hard stare, his eyes suddenly cold under his straight black brows.

"To live here, you mean?" he asked slowly. "Aunt Anne is this so?"

At her nod, he swung away, crossing the room quickly, the stiffened skirts of his brocade coat swaying with each step.

44

Reaching his aunt, he bent over her, talking urgently into her ear and Anna could only catch the disjointed murmur of his words.

The older woman reached up and patted his hand reassuringly. "Have no fear, nephew," she said in a normal tone, obviously wanting Anna to hear, and looking across the room, she smiled into her anxious countenance. "Miss Anna, I am sure can be relied upon to be discreet. If there are things that puzzle her in the household, then I know she will have the good manners and good sense to ignore them — besides, James, she has a decided preference with regard to flowers." She raised her voice and called across the room meaningly. "I was just telling my nephew, Miss Anna, that of all the flowers in our English gardens you are loyal to the white rose."

"That is so," Anna answered gravely, accepting the lead given her. "I prefer it to all others."

The young man scarcely spared her a glance, all his attention centred on the woman beside him. "Aunt, I would remind you that we are expecting visitors

45

and, while not wishing to appear churlish or unwelcoming to Miss Stanton, at the moment I do not feel that we can offer her hospitality."

Lady Primrose pulled her needlework table closer to her elbow and placidly began to sort the tangle of silks it contained. "I arrange my household, nephew," she said mildly.

At her words James let out a sharp breath, and turned abruptly away to stare across the room at Anna. Meeting his eyes blandly, she smiled slightly, doing her best to give the impression that she had been unaware of the hurried conversation and hidden emotions.

"Faw! You're a dull, old stick brother James," cried his sister, hurrying into the breach. "Take no notice, Miss Stanton, his mood is ever uncertain. In fact, he probably wishes to fill the house with his own friends."

"I have no wish to cause trouble — shall we leave the matter for a while to give you time to think it over again?"

"No such thing," put in Lady Primrose, intent upon the silks on her lap. "The position is arranged. We'd be grateful if you would come as soon as possible."

Anna allowed herself to glance from face to face of the occupants of the room. "I-if you are sure."

"Quite sure, my dear," said Lady Primrose firmly. "Now, James, Miss Anna will wish to return to her lodgings — if you will be good enough to escort her."

While awaiting the arrival of a sedan-chair, arrangements were made that she should return as soon as Kit had left to join his regiment and, with the affectionate farewells of the young Irish girl ringing in her ears, Anna left the elegant house in Essex Street in the unusual luxury of a 'chair'. Stealing a glance from time to time at her escort as he walked beside her, Anna could not but notice the preoccupied frown beneath the shadow of his tricorn hat. His white wig accentuated the tan of his face, proclaiming that he spent many hours out of doors and she felt a growing interest as she speculated upon his habits; realising that here was no fashionable fop, who spent most of his time in the salons and card rooms of society, but one whose air spoke of a man of action. Involuntarily she was reminded of Captain Bellamy, though in precisely what way, she could not say.

Suddenly the young man looked up and catching her eyes upon him, his brow cleared as though by magic and he smiled.

"What a boor you must think me," he said ruefully, leaning towards the window of the sedan.

Nonplussed Anna gazed at him, nibbling her lip as she sought for some suitable disclaimer; if she had not been aware of the reason behind his dislike of her staying at Essex Street she would undoubtedly have thought him the worst of boors.

"Not at all," she said politely at last, as the carrying men turned into Green Square and set the sedan-chair down outside her lodgings.

Mr Drelincourt helped her to alight, but retained his grip on her hand a little longer than was necessary. "My apologies, Miss Stanton," he said quietly as the men walked away. "My only excuse is the fact that I feel the cares of being the only man of my family. You must realise that my sister is charming, but without a thought in her head save the newest fashion or the latest gossip and my aunt . . . is wealthy and easily put-upon."

Feeling Anna's withdrawal at his frankness, he tightened his grasp on her fingers, covering her hand with both of his.

"I'll confess that at first I suspected that you might be an adventuress, eager to hang upon my aunt's goodness and — forgive me, but it was for that reason that I appeared unwelcoming. However I have only to look into your face to see the honesty and goodness there and to know how mistaken I was in my assumption." He smiled down at her disarmingly. "Pray forgive me," he begged.

Staring up at him, suddenly aware of his devastating charm, Anna blinked, glanced away and decided she must accept his apology at its face value.

"Willingly," she said and allowed him to carry her hand to his lips.

He smiled disarmingly and allowed her to feel the full force of his blue gaze as he bent over her. "We shall meet again shortly," he said, "but in the meantime, my sister and I walk in the park about mid-morning — may I hope to see you and your brother there?"

Anna nodded. "That would be delightful," she said, "though, to be honest I don't know when Kit will be leaving to join his regiment."

"Then, let us make arrangements for tomorrow," he suggested going on quickly when she hesitated. "I am sure he will wish to meet his sister's new friends and to satisfy himself that we will take good care of you."

Having to acknowledge this, Anna agreed and James Drelincourt took his leave, leaving her to climb the steep stairs to her lodgings, suddenly weary after the events of the last hours.

A man turned his head from contemplation of the street below as she entered and, blinded by the dim light in the room after the bright spring sunshine, she at first took him for Kit and started forward, her hands out in welcome, before stopping in consternation halfway across the room, as the set of his shoulders and height told her that he was not her brother.

"A very pretty scene," commented Captain Bellamy, drily. "I see you have managed to add James Drelincourt to your list of beaus."

Anna dropped her hat onto the polished table top and turned away, her wide hoops swinging. "Was not that what you wanted?" she asked coldly.

"I had not imagined you so adroit at the task."

"Oh, I found it relatively easy to worm my way into their house and confidence. They seem very nice, gullible people — I've even been offered a position as companion to Cecilia Drelincourt. I daresay that given a little time I shall be able to open the door at night to thieves or even arrange to have Cessy abducted if that's your wish — "

"It might be."

His harsh words cut across her angry voice and she stopped abruptly and looked at him, her eyes suddenly wide and still. "W-what do you mean?" she asked, shaken.

"That whatever I require, be it distasteful

or merely bewildering, I shall expect your implicit obedience. There is no room for half-hearted compliance in my employ, Miss Stanton. Do you understand?"

"Oh, yes. I understand," she said, bitterly, "but I'd find it very hard to stab or shoot someone."

"You have seen too many melodramas," he commented drily. "I would never ask you to do anything so clumsy . . . our methods are much subtler than that." He stood up from the windowseat, flicking out the lace at his wrists. "Rest assured, my dear, I have no intention at the moment of asking you to perform so drastic an action. But I do require your word that you will perform any other little task I may ask of you."

Taking her arm, he swung her round to face him, turning up her face with a careless finger under her chin.

"They are nice people!" she burst out, shaking herself free.

"And I am not." He smiled a little, standing so close that she would have liked to step back, but was prevented from doing so by the table behind her. "Nevertheless I will have your word."

"No."

His eyes glinted reminding her of a chill winter's day. "Remember Kit," he advised quietly, holding her gaze, "and give me your word, for what it's worth."

For a moment she struggled with herself, trying to find the moral courage to refuse him and, perhaps if it had been for herself alone she might have found it, but the thought of Kit, degraded and despairing in a debtor's prison was more than she could bear and dropping her eyes, she gave in.

"V-very well," she sighed, her shoulders drooping as she picked at the broken flowers on her ruined hat.

Captain Bellamy watched her closely for a moment, before shrugging slightly, he turned away to the window again.

"How did you manage to inveigle an invitation to stay the night at Essex Street?" he asked with little interest, his attention directed to the street below.

"The doctor advised it," she replied listlessly.

He looked up quickly. "Doctor?"

Anna looked at him. "Something on

the coach cut my hand," she told him evenly. "I supposed it part of your plan — and was only grateful that it did not require something more drastic."

His gaze was cold. "Don't snivel, miss. The life you lead must be dangerous — and care was taken that you did not sustain hurt."

"I can well believe that to have me lying with a broken leg would be of little use to you." Remembrance of the fright she had sustained returned and her voice shook with indignation, while she grew chill at his indifference.

Something in the street had attracted his attention and he gestured to her suddenly. "Kit," he explained. "Pray compose yourself. Tell him only that which is necessary and *nothing* of our arrangements."

Pressing her into a chair by the fireplace, he leaned his arm along the mantelpiece and by the time Kit arrived in the room the scene was one of calm.

" . . . such an adventure," Captain Bellamy was saying, breaking off at the younger man's entry to exclaim, "My dear Kit, have you heard your sister's tale? I vow such driving should not be allowed. Do you see the rogue actually cut her hand."

"Cut? Are you hurt, Anna?" asked her brother quickly, crossing the room swiftly and taking up her bandaged hand. "I thought from the message that you were merely shaken."

"J-just a little cut, I do assure you," Anna said. "Nothing to worry about. The doctor did all that was right and proper, and everyone has been most sympathetic." She could not avoid sending Captain Bellamy a malicious glance.

"And those people — the Drelincourts? What of them?"

Anna smiled at his anxious tones. "Why, brother," she said sweetly, "had I known you to be so worried, I would have expected a visit from you last night."

Kit had the grace to hang his head. "I would have come, Ann, indeed I would, but the thing is that by the time I came in and read the message it was too late to call on anyone."

Touching his arm lightly, she promised

not to tease him any more and went on to explain the circumstances of her acquaintance with the family in Essex Street, reminding him of their mother's friendship with Lady Primrose.

"Well, how convenient!" he marvelled. "Everything has worked out splendidly. To own the truth I was a little bothered over how you would manage without me. It's not at all the thing for a lady to live alone, you know."

"I'm sure our landlady would prove a dragon of a duenna," Anna commented demurely, going on before she should forget. "I hope you have no arrangements for tomorrow morning, Kit. James Drelincourt has invited us to meet himself and his sister in the park."

"Rafe and I had thought of — "

"I would be delighted to take a turn in the park," put in the older man, swinging his quizzing glass from its long black ribbon. "I fancy I have a slight acquaintance with James Drelincourt." He bowed in Anna's direction. "If Miss Stanton has no objection, of course."

"Anna doesn't mind," said her brother, "why should she?"

Anna was forced to smile her compliance, while reflecting that she would have preferred the soldier's absence, owing to a feeling that the meeting of James Drelincourt and Captain Bellamy would be like the clashing of two opposites. Still puzzled by the illusive likeness she detected between them, she turned her head to look at the man beside her and was disconcerted to find his grey glance full upon her. For a moment their eyes locked as he deliberately held her gaze, before turning back to Kit he continued their conversation.

Considerably shaken Anna leaned back against the chair.; the chilling gaze had been inimical and yet full of warning and above all so cold and ruthless that she had been struck anew by apprehension and a growing fear for what the future might hold.

3

MAY was in, the milkmaids had been seen in the streets wearing their Mayday garlands a few days before and ignoring the old adage, Anna shook out the petticoats of her sprigged silk gown to wear to the park. Tying the ribbons of her wide, leghorn hat under her chin, she surveyed her reflection in the spotted glass of the mirror in her bedchamber, and knew that she looked her best.

Muted voices carried to her from the stairwell and she paused in easing on her long leather gloves to listen, before taking up her reticule she left the room to join her brother and his visitor.

As she had supposed Captain Bellamy was with him in the parlour and both men broke off their conversation to turn to her as she entered.

"Why Ann how grand you are!" Kit exclaimed, obviously a little startled by her appearance. "Do you intend to impress your new friends?"

"I vow you'll outshine the flowers in the park," put in the soldier gallantly, bowing slightly.

Anna shot him a look of dislike and turned to her brother. "I wouldn't like them to think me a country nobody," she told him crisply. "You are so fine, I would hardly match with you in my old gown."

Uneasily aware of the amount he had spent on his own clothes Kit made haste to make amends. "They are sure to think you one of the aristocracy," he said, hoping to flatter her.

Anna laughed. "As long as they don't think me too fine to be Miss Drelincourt's companion — "

They soon set out for the park and, out of politeness, Anna had to accept Captain Bellamy's offer of his arm. Suddenly aware of his unaccustomed nearness, and feeling dwarfed by his height, she could feel his strength as her hand rested lightly on his velvet-covered arm, and for some reason was thrown into confusion. Doing her best to hide her nervousness, she began to talk quickly upon any matter that came into her head, aware that she was prattling but unable to remain silent.

"*So* much more noisy than the country," agreed her companion, shielding her from the rough passage of an errand boy and, meeting his eyes, Anna was mortified to see the amusement in their depths and realised that he was very well aware of the reason for her inconsequential chatter.

Biting her lip, she fell silent and would have withdrawn her hand from the crook of his elbow, but strong fingers closed unobtrusively over hers and held her prisoner. After a moment's silent struggle, she was forced to acknowledge him the victor and throwing him a stormy glance, met his bland gaze.

"Where are these friends of yours to be met?" enquired her brother, unaware of the battle that had been enacted beside him.

"The l–long walk, Mr Drelincourt said."

Alerted by her stutter, Kit glanced down at her. "Don't be nervous Anna," he said kindly. "Rafe and I are here — we won't let the Irish eat you."

Cecilia and James were found admiring a stone fountain, introductions and bows were exchanged and somehow Anna found herself hanging onto James Drelincourt's arm, while Captain Bellamy performed a like service for his sister. Suspecting that the soldier had arranged matters to his own satisfaction, she sent him an expressive glance to receive a bland smile in return, before he bent his head attentively over his companion and a somewhat chagrined Kit was forced to fall in beside a young man who had been with the Irish couple.

Discovering that he was on furlough from his regiment Kit brightened considerably and spent a very pleasant morning, discovering the joys to be expected from a life in the army, while Anna did her best to create a good impression with the young Irishman as she strained to hear what Captain Bellamy was saying to Cecilia.

Suddenly realising that Mr Drelincourt had fallen silent and was obviously awaiting her reply, she apologised prettily and begged him to repeat his question.

"I asked if you ever attended the

theatre, Miss Stanton. My sister and I have a great liking for it."

"The only plays I have ever seen were performed by travelling players," she told him candidly, "which I cannot believe are anything like a London company."

"And did you enjoy your play?"

Looking back she could remember the excitement of the country audience and almost smell the guttering candles and greasepaint. "Oh, indeed I did," she exclaimed, recalling the anticipation and exhilaration she had felt as the story was unfolded.

"Cessy and I are arranging a theatre party — would you and your brother care to come?"

"I should like it above all things!" Her gaze fell on her brother and recalling his imminent departure, her eyes clouded. "But I don't know if Kit will be here."

"Ah, yes, he's waiting to join his regiment. In that case, we must be quick with our arrangements."

But as it happened, having spent much time at his tailors, Kit was called to join his regiment the day before the planned outing. Messages were sent back and forth and it was arranged that Anna should take up residence in Essex Street the day of his departure to accompany the Drelincourts to the theatre from her new home.

"It's a good thing, Ann," said Kit seriously. "It will take your mind away from worrying over me."

He pivoted, and craned his neck, the better to see the back of his new uniform that he was trying on, ostensibly for his sister's benefit. Anna blinked at the red and gold magnificence, staring up at the young face, almost unrecognisable under the formal white wig.

"I would hardly know you," she said slowly, her eyes travelling over his slender figure. "You look quite different."

Kit preened a little and shook out the lace ruffles at his wrists in a manner learned from Captain Bellamy and tried his black tricorn at a new angle. "There's no doubt that a uniform becomes a man," he observed, obviously pleased with his reflection and looking at the stranger before her, Anna had to agree; gone was the slim, almost foppish figure of the last few months and in his place was a young man with an air of resolution.

"It's what I've always wanted to do, you know Ann," Kit said, unconsciously squaring his shoulders. "I'll do my best, now I've the opportunity."

Accepting the unspoken promise, Anna cast all thoughts of gambling and uncertainties aside and smiled up at him. "I know you will, my love," she said with certainty and going to him, reached up and placed a kiss on his cheek. "I'm proud of you Christopher and I know mother and father would have been as well."

Seeing his air of artless pride and satisfaction her promise to Captain Bellamy seemed worthwhile and she deliberately put aside all thought of the duplicity of her actions with regard to the Drelincourts, telling herself that she was acting out of loyalty to King George. However when she arrived at Essex Street she was received with such warmth and kindness that all her doubts were renewed and she was filled with guilty unease.

Restless and unhappy she sat in front of her dressing table, staring blindly at the reflection in the mirror and was so long in dressing for the theatre that Cecilia came in search of her.

"We will miss the prologue," she warned, advancing into the room, her silk skirts rustling and stopped at the sight of the other's shadowed eyes. "To be sure and I'd forgotten how worried you'd be over your brother," she exclaimed, mistaking the cause for Anna's unhappiness. "Forgive me for such thoughtlessness, won't you?"

She gave the other girl an impetuous hug and Anna forced herself to smile. "Are we late? My apologies — I'd forgot the time, I'm afraid."

Standing up, she shook out her petticoats, hoping that no-one would recognise her sprigged silk gown and hastily dabbed perfume on her wrists. "There, I'm ready," she said and turned with a deliberately bright smile.

A familiar figure in pale satin turned as they came down the stairs and Anna faltered at Captain Bellamy's elaborate bow.

"We thought you'd like a familiar escort," whispered the Irish girl, squeezing her hand. "We asked him to make up numbers when we heard that your brother could not be here."

"It's very kind of you, but — " she hesitated a little uncertain how to phrase her words, "but Captain Bellamy is really more Kit's friend than mine."

She thought Cecilia looked faintly relieved but her expression was fleeting and as they reached the hall at that moment and the maids ran forward with their cloaks, she could not be certain.

Several other couples had been invited to make up the party and in the flurry of introductions and greetings, Anna forgot her worry and suddenly found she was enjoying the attentions of James Drelincourt and the young soldier she had met a few days previously.

"Jason Weston, here, is sure you must have a decided preference for military men," the Irishman declared.

"I am informed upon the best authority that a uniform does something for a man," she rejoined. "My brother told me so, having tried on his regimentals for the first time."

Her voice was unconsciously wistful and she sighed a little at the thought of her brother setting out on his new life. Seeing her downcast expression the men seized upon the opportunity to cheer her, each trying to outdo the other in their attempts to raise her spirits. Their infectious gaiety was catching and soon Anna found herself smiling at their drolleries and trying to sharpen her wits on theirs. The presence of Captain Bellamy was the only stay upon the lightness of her spirits, the sight of his violet clad shoulders among the other guests, stilling her laughter and filling her with a sobriety which she tried to hide.

Somewhat to her relief he appeared to have eyes and attention only for Cecilia Drelincourt, and when the sedan-chairs arrived for the ladies, took up position beside the Irish girl as though by right. Some of the younger men would have opposed him, but the set of his broad shoulders and air of authority gave them pause and eventually he was left in sole possession by the side of Cessy's sedan.

Link boys marching ahead with their flaming torches, the little cortège moved off, Anna finding herself escorted by

James Drelincourt and Mr Weston on either side.

Drury Lane was a hive of activity, with coaches arriving outside the theatre and sedan-chairs depositing their occupants on the shallow steps. Anna stepped out of her chair and barely had time to shake out her skirts before her arm was taken and she was escorted among the milling crowds and along the narrow passage to the box reserved for the Drelincourt party.

Her first glimpse of the interior filled her with amazement; huge ring-like chandeliers hung from the ceiling, candles striking dazzling sparks from their glass lustres. Yellow and gold paint added to the opulence of the scene, while the boxes on either side of the stage were hung with red velvet drapery.

Having taken in the scene around and beside her, Anna glanced over the edge of the box, attracted by the loud hum, sounding like the drone from an enormous beehive, that arose from below. To her amazement, the space below her gaze was filled with myriads of people all talking and moving, appearing to her country eyes as if most of London had decided to go to the theatre.

The ladies took their places upon the slender chairs provided, while the gentlemen ranged themselves behind. Soon the curtain rose and the audience gave a murmur of anticipation. Used as she was to the histrionics displayed by the travelling players whom she had seen in her home town, at first Anna was bothered by the understated acting of David Garrick, but soon his quiet gestures and natural voice had charmed her and she was lost in the spell spun around the audience by the actor.

The air was heavy with the smell of melting wax, burning wicks and cloying perfume. Going to Anna's head like a drug, it intoxicated her with excitement, while the play and unusual surroundings filled her with exhilaration. As the curtain fell for the last time, she sighed with happiness and sank back in her chair, her eyes aglow, almost unwilling to return to reality.

"No need to ask if you enjoyed the play," observed James Drelincourt, looking down at her flushed face.

"No, indeed — such naturalness, such normal tones," she enthused, confiding that for the first time she could feel sympathy for Hamlet, rather than irritation for his melancholy.

"I find him a poor fellow," James confessed, taking her arm and leading her from the box. "I've a liking for bold, brave adventurers, I'm afraid. Men who venture all on the toss of a coin — or for the love of a lady."

Anna glanced up quickly, wondering if the Jacobite cause came into this category, but found his gaze above her head as he nodded to some acquaintance across the crowd. For a moment she stared at his handsome profile, the shadows from the flickering candles dancing over his tanned features, before she dropped her eyes and looked away hastily, afraid he would become aware of her gaze.

Beside his orange satin suit, decorated with silver embroidery, she suddenly felt drab and uninteresting in her old silk gown and longed wildly for fashionable clothes and the beauty to attract her companion, not realising that her quiet good looks and unconscious air of elegance were attraction enough among the over-dressed, affected women to whom he was used.

The journey home was quickly accomplished and the party spilled into the large dining-room of the house in Essex Street, where a cold meal had been set out. Anna seated herself in one of the deep window embrasures, half hidden by the velvet curtain, content for the minute to think about the play and idly watch the gay company.

Suddenly her thoughts were interrupted by a voice above her and she looked up to meet the equivocal gaze of Captain Bellamy.

"I've taken the liberty of procuring you some supper," he said, placing a plate on her lap.

"H-how kind!" Anna was startled by this unexpected act of gallantry, before she realised that, as with all the soldier's actions, it must mask some ulterior motive. "I gather you wish to speak to me," she went on coolly, recovering her composure.

Captain Bellamy raised one eyebrow. "My dear Miss Stanton, I deplore your lack of finesse — a little light conversation, a slight air of flirtation to allay any suspicions and *then* to business."

Anna eyed him coldly, noting the red breaking through the light scattering of powder in his hair, the elegant suit he wore, the froth of Mechlin lace at his wrists and throat, his air of debonair attentiveness as he bent over her, before her gaze returned to his face and she read the cold, grey eyes behind the laughing expression.

Unable to suppress a shiver, she looked away, the food suddenly tasteless in her mouth. "What do you want?" she asked dully.

"You look quite pale — shall I open the window?" Suiting the words to actions, he reached behind her and flung the casement open, letting in a wave of cool air and setting the candles flickering.

Involuntarily people glanced in their direction and as though by chance, he stepped in front of the girl shielding her from their gaze. Taking the fan from its string round her wrist he flipped it open and began to wave it gently.

"Miss Stanton is a little overcome by the heat," he explained quietly to Cecilia who was standing near. "Do not, I pray, concern yourself, she is feeling better already."

"Anna? Shall I take you to your room?" enquired the Irish girl anxiously.

"N-no — it's nothing. Truly I am better now."

"A little walk in the garden would do you good. Captain Bellamy, pray take her out onto the terrace."

Bowing gallantly, he tucked her hand under his arm, and aware of the many eyes upon her, Anna had to accompany him into the dark garden. Once out of sight, she removed her arm and moved away from her companion, leaning against the low balustrade and staring out over the black lawn and trees, the smell of damp earth carrying to her nostrils and making her long for the country with an unexpected fervour.

"What is it?" he asked, hearing her sigh. "How I wish we had never left the country," she said vehemently. "That my father had not died and that Kit and I were still at home in the vicarage — that

73

neither of us had ever met you!"

He was silent so long a time, his shoulder turned to her that, at last she stole a glance at him, half frightened of what she would see on his face, but his expression was unfathomable.

"We all wish that life might have been otherwise," he said bleakly, leaving her to wonder if she had heard aright, when he went on in quite a different tone.

"Now to business, before we arouse gossip with the length of our absence."

Anna was surprised that he should care about so mundane a thing as reputation, but upon reflection realised that he would wish to appear as conventional as most.

"You are cultivating our Mr Drelincourt, I see, which, of course, is what I want you to do, but don't be too obvious in it. Play him like a fish, without him being aware of it. Let him become used to you and your presence in this house, until he ceases to be wary and on his guard. *Then* lead him into indiscretions of secrecy — it should be easy to ask artless questions, while passing yourself off as a fervent Jacobite."

Hanging her head, Anna wondered

miserably if this could be true, if such improbable happenings were real, hoping that she would suddenly awaken and find herself back in her bed at Alstead.

"Yes, this is a dirty business, Miss Stanton," Captain Bellamy said harshly, putting a hand under her chin to jerk her head up. "From now on you are not nice to know. You'll cheat and betray people who are your friends, people who have been kind to you. You'll be in bed at night hating yourself, but most of all, my dear Anna, you'll be afraid — afraid that that young fanatic will find you out and afraid of me." His pale eyes bored down into hers, holding her gaze with the intensity of his own. "Believe me, my dear, it would be very foolish to even think of duping me! and whatever else you might be, I am persuaded that you are not a fool."

Anna swallowed convulsively, while sick fear cramped her stomach and made her tremble. Only to herself would she admit her fright and lifting her chin out of his grasp, she faced the soldier defiantly.

"I know quite well how low is the

trade of a spy," she almost whispered, her voice shaking despite her attempt to steady it, "for I have an example before me. I am well aware, Captain Bellamy, how despicable is your business — and how lacking you are in all that others call honour!"

Shaking with emotion, she turned away from him, and almost ran towards the door into the house, blundering into someone in the entrance.

"Hold hard! Miss Stanton — is aught amiss? Surely Bellamy has not — ?"

Looking up into James Drelincourt's astonished face, Anna shook her head and tried to smile. "It's nothing," she assured him breathlessly. "Pray don't concern yourself."

"But what is it? You are trembling. Has something frightened you?"

"N-no — nothing. The heat . . . I felt a little faint. Oh, *please*," she begged as he still seemed inclined to pursue the matter, "please don't make a fuss."

For a moment he looked steadily down at her, his blue eyes searching her face. Apparently satisfied at last, he threaded her hand through the crook of his elbow, holding her arm reassuringly. "I'll take your word, Miss Anna," he said softly, leading her back into the crowded room, "but believe me when I say that I am ever at your service. With your brother away and you living here with us, I shall constitute myself your guardian — and make your welfare my concern. If anyone annoys you in any way, don't hesitate to tell me — rest assured that my methods will be discreet."

Anna thanked him, maliciously pleased that Captain Bellamy should be suspected of making advances to her and deliberately suppressing the fear that the soldier engendered in her, put on a cloak of gaiety, determined to appear to enjoy what was left of the evening.

Sometime later, she was laughing kindly at a rather laboured witticism of Ensign Weston, when a name rose above the hum of conversation and carried to her ears as if spoken directly to her. Startled, she glanced around trying to identify the speaker, while still appearing to give the young soldier her attention. At last she settled upon a group around Lady Primrose some yards distant. Closer together and more serious than the other conversationalists, their avid and yet grave air, confirmed her suspicions and still so talking to Jason Weston she slowly and carefully edged nearer.

" . . . of course our day will come. There can be no doubt of that," Lady Primrose was saying positively and Anna strained her ears to hear more.

"The whole country is restless. There is talk of rebellion in all quarters," said a gentleman unknown to Anna.

"Not rebellion, Sir John," corrected Lady Primrose's nephew. "The Stuarts are the rightful kings of England. I would have you remember that the Hanoverian Elector is the usurper."

"Of course, of course," agreed the older man hastily, startled by Mr Drelincourt's aggression.

"Sir John knows quite well who is who," soothed Lady Primrose, a hand warningly on her nephew's arm. "Remember, James, it is as well to practise a little discretion."

"Discretion!" snorted the disgusted young man. "I am tired of discretion, what we need is action."

"We saw enough of that in forty five," Sir John reminded him a little sourly.

"Not enough," retorted James fiercely. "Or, by God, a Stuart King would be sitting now where fat George puts his rump."

Several heads had turned at the sound of raised voices and James Drelincourt swallowed his ire and began a long, involved tale of his travels on the continent, abandoning it as soon as his guests' attention had faded.

"Pray fetch me a glass of lemonade," Anna begged Ensign Weston, suddenly recalling his presence and wishing to hide her own interest in her hostess' conversation. As the young man retreated upon his errand, she turned back to the group beside her, aware that once again they were intent upon serious matters.

"Dr King at Oxford," Lady Primrose was explaining and Anna had to wait impatiently for her own enlightenment.

"The fellow's a fool," exclaimed Sir John. "Making an exhibition of himself!"

"I am inclined to agree with you," James admitted quietly, but his aunt broke in, her eyes shining.

"I think it wonderful," she said. "That a man should be so sure in his allegiance that he could make a Jacobite speech in the college, arouse his listeners to enthusiasm and make clear his own sentiments. How brave — how truly brave!"

"If he's arrested he'll be of little use to us," James pointed out.

"Not a moment ago you were wishing for action," complained Sir John irritably, "now, when someone shows his true colours — "

"Action, yes, but only when it's of use to the cause, not in rabble rousing speeches which only draw attention to us!"

"At least we're having action in Paris," broke in Lady Primrose pacifically. "I hear the White Rose has grown suddenly wealthy."

Anna allowed her eyes to search the room unobtrusively, wondering if Captain Bellamy was within listening distance, but not finding him among the moving, talking throng, decided that he must have left the house.

As though mention of money made

them more discreet, the group behind Anna drew closer together and their conversation fell to a whisper of which she could only catch a few disjointed words, which made little sense. Catching sight of the returning Ensign, bearing a glass of yellow liquid, she decided to abandon any attempt to hear the sibilant murmurs behind her and went to join him.

"Have you heard of a Dr King of Oxford?" she asked, absently sipping her drink and felt a little surprised when the young man nodded an affirmative.

"Yes — if you mean the Principal of St Mary's Hall, that is and not some quack who happens to live in Oxford."

Anna was interested. "I should think the one I mean is the Principal," she said. "Do you know anything else about him?"

"If my brother hadn't come down from Oxford I wouldn't have known that . . . though I have heard that he made a speech at the opening of Radcliffe which excited comment."

Feigning loss of interest Anna yawned politely behind her hand and sighed that she hadn't a head for politics, hoping that it would dispel any suspicions her questions might have aroused, and turned the conversation in other directions, asking after her companion's career.

"At the moment I am on half-pay," he told her, "but soon shall rejoin my regiment before we leave for America."

"America!" she exclaimed, remembering all the tales she had heard of the country on the other side of the world.

"The unknown Continent," he went on enthusiastically. "Almost unexplored, with forests and land that no-one has set foot upon save the red savages."

"H-how can you be so happy?" she demanded indignantly. "Think of your poor family when you are away, worrying over what might be happening to you."

He laughed ruefully. "My poor family, Miss Stanton, consists of an elder brother with a young brood of his own to concern him, and my dear Mama, is a widow with a clutch of daughters to launch upon the world. They will think of me occasionally, but I am sure they will have other worries to occupy their minds."

Rather taken aback at this unexpected

view of a large family, Anna smiled uncertainly, remarking that she was sure he did his mother an injustice.

"Upon my word, she'll be more intent upon finding Lizzie a husband or upon wondering if the striped brocade or the embroidered silk is more suitable for Mary."

"Now, what is going on here?" demanded a voice from behind them. "I vow you look quite thunderstruck."

Anna turned to Cecilia and made the content of the conversation known to her.

"Well, upon my word," declared the Irish girl, "we can't have such a thing — half a world away and no-one to think of him, indeed." Impulsively she turned to the other girl. "You and I, Anna, shall take on the task. There, Mr Weston we give you our word that sometime each day we shall recall your face and wish you well."

With a grave air and a touching attempt at gallantry, Jason Weston bowed and kissed their hands. "What more should I need to keep me safe? I shall be impervious to attack from both French and Indians."

"Do you like Jason Weston?" Cecilia asked hesitantly, much later when the guests had left and the girls paused on the landing outside Anna's room

"He seems a nice young man," Anna replied, cautiously.

"You — don't care for Captain Bellamy?"

Staring at the other in amazement, she realised that the Irish girl was asking delicately if there was an attachment between herself and the soldier.

"Indeed, no," she answered quickly and realising that her reply had been too vehement, went on more calmly. "Rafe Bellamy is my brother's friend, not mine . . . I c-could wish that he wasn't Kit's crony."

"You don't like him?"

Anna looked away. "I don't feel he's good for Kit — he's older, for one thing and I feel too much a man of the world to befriend a boy of my brother's age."

Cecilia was silent. "I — rather like him," she said lightly. "I might see if I can make him my beau — it would be interesting to see if the gallant Captain has a heart."

"Oh, don't!" Anna exclaimed involuntarily and realised from the other's expression that she should qualify her hasty words. "I mean — I feel sure that Captain Bellamy is a hard man. I don't think he would be kind. Cessy — I am afraid you would be hurt."

"Tush!" exclaimed the other, laughing. "I assure you that I can take care of myself and know better than to give my heart to one who has no desire for it."

Suddenly Anna felt younger than the blonde girl, aware for the first time that Cecilia Drelincourt had been about in the social world much longer than she and smiled at her knowledgeable tone.

"Oh, Cecilia!" she exclaimed, "and *I* am supposed to chaperon you."

"I promise not to be too difficult," laughed the other girl and hurried along the corridor to her bedchamber, leaving Anna to watch her retreating figure and wonder with much misgiving at what the future might hold; she suddenly suspected that even without the distraction provided by Rafe Bellamy, the chaperoning of Miss Drelincourt might prove more than a little difficult.

4

ANNA was still not used to the luxury of being woken by a maid with a cup of hot chocolate and lay for a moment the next morning contemplating the change in her situation, before lifting herself against the high nest of pillows, she reached for the silver mug, left beside the bed.

As she drank her eyes wandered around the elegant room, its walls covered in pale blue brocaded paper. Material of the same colour was drapped from the tall posts of her bed and hung at the window. The maid had drawn back the curtains before she left and Anna could see a branch from a cherry tree nodding against the window, its soft pink blossoms just opening.

Slipping from the bed, she crossed to the tall window, gazing out at the garden below, marvelling that a town house could possess such a haven of greenness. The terrace gave access to a formal oblong lawn, bounded with regimented flower beds, just now filled with spring flowers while beyond that rustic arbours gave onto a fashionable 'wilderness' of shrubs and trees, with stone statues and seats, strategically placed for tête-à-têtes or whispered secrets. The encircling walls were hidden by roses or climbing fruit trees which softened the hard outline of red brick and made the occupants of the garden hardly aware of being enclosed.

Recalling that she and Cecilia were to go shopping that morning and happily aware of the purse Lady Primrose had given her previously as advance upon her wages as chaperon, Anna hurriedly completed her toilet. Reflecting that the old rose pink taffeta which she had spent many laborious hours turning and restitching, really had turned out quite well, she smoothed her hair and settled the wisp of lace which covered the knot of curls on top of her head, before hurrying from the room.

Sometime later the two girls, accompanied by Betty, Cecilia's maid, set out towards the Strand and the delights of 'The Exchange', the enormous shop that could be counted upon to stock and sell anything a fashionable lady might desire.

As the weather was fine and their destination not far distant, they had declined the use of a coach or sedan-chair and set out on foot and finding much to occupy their conversation, arrived happily in the Strand.

Cecilia and her maid went at once in search of some lavender coloured gloves, leaving Anna to make a slow circuit of the counters, planning how best to spend her money. She soon realised that what had seemed like a prodigious amount to her country eyes, in fact could not be stretched too far and she reluctantly said farewell to the gown of white sarsenet she had dreamed about, settling instead for one length of cream silk and two shorter ones of apricot and blue to make petticoats that she hoped would change the appearance of the new gown. Making a careful selection of ribbons and knots and trimmings to add new life to the wardrobe she already had, she passed on to choose a pair of gloves, knowing that no fashionable lady would be without a pair of the softest, palest kid and there met Cecilia, torn between the rival merits of two shades of lavender kid.

"And they have different perfumes!" she wailed in mock despair. "I vow one smells of roses and the other of musk. Help me to choose, Anna, dear."

The other studied the gloves, pointed out that the stitching was not quite so fine on one as the other and minded the Irish girl that with summer coming rose scent was sure to be the more desirable.

"Sure and what would I do without you?" cried Cessy, happily accepting her decision and paying for her purchase.

"Now, I declare that's the very thing to brighten up my old blue satin gown," she declared on their way out, stopping beside a counter that displayed imitation flowers and pointing to an elaborate orange spray made of curling feathers.

"It won't set off your hair," Anna pointed out.

"Poof — it's just the thing and I'm determined to have it — with that pinned to my corsage no-one will notice that they've seen the dress before."

Repressing a faint shudder, Anna

agreed with her, hoping that the monstrous object might be mislaid or discarded.

"Now, I must buy you a present," Cecilia went on, refusing all disclaimers from the other and desiring the counter clerk to reach down a full-blown pink rose.

"I'd liefer have the spray of white rose-buds," said Anna quietly, seeing it would hurt the other's feelings to refuse the gift and taking the opportunity to assert her Jacobite leanings.

"Indeed?" Cecilia's blue eyes opened wide as she stared at her companion for a moment. "To be sure, I had forgot that you had a liking for flowers of that colour."

"Only r-roses," Anna reminded her gently, returning the gaze, "as I believe you have yourself." The Irish girl looked a little discomposed, but quickly recovered herself. "Oh, I daresay you'll find white roses in my aunt's garden," she said with a light laugh, "but as for myself I like all colours. I confess to having no preference."

Pondering upon the other's statement, Anna followed her into the street again, wondering if she had been politely warned away from politics, or if Cecilia really had no political leanings and had told her so.

"Carry your parcels, miss?" whined a voice by her shoulder as she stepped into the street and Anna looked to see a roughly dressed, undersized urchin waiting hopefully by her elbow and was about to shake her head when he accosted her again.

"Go on, miss, you can trust me. Any messages to be run — or such like?"

Something in his voice caught her interest and she looked at him more closely, taking in his appearance and general air of expectancy.

"D-do I know you?" she asked, puzzled.

The boy shook his head. "Don't think so, miss," he answered cheerfully. "Ben Bow's the name. On account of me being found on the steps of Bow Bells."

"You're a foundling?"

"Yes, miss. Ain't got no mother nor father and has to earn me own living — every penny helps, miss," he reminded her hopefully.

Anna searched in her pocket, amused by his frankness. "Here's a penny," she said, dropping the coin into his open palm. "You can have it on account."

"Account of what, miss?" asked the boy, running alongside her, as she hurried to join Cecilia who was waiting a little way along the street.

"You can owe me an errand," Anna explained, "but now go away."

"Who was that?" Cecilia asked, vaguely interested.

"His name is Ben Bow he says — he's a street boy and was asking for employment. The odd thing is that he seems familiar."

Cecilia glanced over her shoulder. "He looks like one of those youths that knocked you over the other day, when you rescued me from death."

Anna stood still, struck by the other's words. "I do believe you're right!" she declared, gazing after the boy.

"I daresay. I have a good memory for faces," returned the other indifferently, losing interest as she returned to the more exciting topic of her new purchases. "I've been thinking," she went on, "about that orange decoration I bought. I believe you are right about it not being quite the thing to go with my blue . . . it would look much better with my green satin."

"I'm sure you are right," agreed Anna, not listening, her thoughts still busy with her new acquaintance; there had been a strange insistence as he emphasised the word 'messages', she decided, wondering if he could have been sent by Captain Bellamy.

Cecilia chatted on happily, unaware of her friend's preoccupation. The streets were a little busier now and it took them longer to reach Essex Street than had the outward journey. They arrived in time to find a large black stallion at the door and James about to mount. Anna's eyes widened at the gallant picture he made, his dark hair unpowdered and wearing a military-style blue velvet coat.

"Oh, James," pouted his sister, as he paused on the steps of the house. "You know I need an escort tomorrow."

"Ask Weston," he advised her briefly, pulling on his gloves and setting his tricorn hat more securely.

"But — where are you going? To

be sure this must be an unexpected journey."

Smiling briefly, he flicked her cheek with one finger.

"Not to me, Cessy," he said, his eyes going beyond her to Anna. "I leave you in good hands. No doubt Miss Stanton will prove a more congenial companion than I."

"Where are you going?" demanded his sister, somewhat petulantly.

"Away on business." He mounted the horse and gathering the reins in his hands, touched his hat to them. "I'll see you anon," he told them, setting heels to the stallion, and Cecilia, who would have held him in conversation had to step back from the flying hooves.

"Well, I do declare!" she exclaimed indignantly. "James is the most vexing person I know . . . and where is he going, I wonder, that is so urgent and secret? There was no mention of a journey last night."

Nibbling her lip, she stared after the retreating figure, before turning on her heel, she ran up the steps with her skirts flying.

"Aunt Anne, Aunt Anne," she called as she entered the house. "Where are you?"

Her aunt's placid voice answered from the small parlour and Cecilia hurried into the room, followed more sedately by her companion.

"Where is James going?" enquired the girl, pulling impatiently at her hat ribbons and tossing that inoffensive article roughly onto a table.

"About some business, I believe," said her aunt calmly. "Why are you so interested?"

"He's the most aggravating creature — he knows I wanted him to escort me to the Pakenham's musical evening tomorrow. Where is he going, anyway — you must know."

"I'm not too sure . . . " said Lady Primrose vaguely, searching among her embroidery threads.

"Oh, Aunt Anne, as though he would have gone without telling you his destination!"

With a hint of exasperation in her expression her aunt looked up, her glance going warningly beyond the Irish girl

95

to Anna standing behind. "You must remember that James is a grown man, Cecilia," she said, "and being of age, has to account to no-one. I daresay if I had asked him, he would have told me where he was going, but I judged it none of my business — and in this case believe it would be best if you so treated it."

Lady Primrose returned to her embroidery and after a moment Cecilia, swung round and left the room, her high heels beating a tattoo expressive of her feelings on the polished wooden floor.

Anna hesitated, wondering if she should go after her, but Lady Primrose looked up, sighing slightly.

"Let her alone," she advised. "All the Drelincourts are cursed with a wild temper, none of them like being thwarted in any way, I'm afraid." She smiled and patted the seat beside her invitingly. "Sit down and talk to me — do you think you will like it with us? Your bedchamber is quite comfortable?"

"It's charming," Anna answered frankly. "When I looked out of the window this morning and saw the garden, I could hardly believe I was in London."

"You're interested in gardening?" asked the older woman quickly, her eyes suddenly alight.

"I can admire and enjoy, but beyond that I'm afraid I have never considered it."

"You should, my dear. It's one of my lasting interests . . . with embroidery. They are both so soothing, so relaxing after life's troubles and worries. I find I have little care for excitement and d — "

She broke off abruptly and leaving the other almost certain she had been about to say 'danger', substituted 'adventure' and went on quickly, with a forced laugh.

"Excitement and adventure — I'd willingly leave them both to you young people."

"I know little enough of either," said Anna quietly, "but I can imagine that one can have too much of them."

"Not, of course, that I've had either in the real meaning of the words," Lady Primrose said hastily, "but life and beaus, finding a husband and so on is exciting enough for any woman."

"Indeed," agreed Anna.

Silence fell in the small room while Lady Primrose took a few quick stitches and Anna was on the point of wondering if she should go, when the older woman spoke again.

"I saw you talking to Jason Weston last evening."

"He seems rather a pleasant person."

The other nodded. "Yes, he comes of a very good family. You need have no fear of being seen with him, but I'm afraid the poor fellow has very little beside his army pay." She smoothed out her work and looked at it critically. "I was talking to Sir John Sligh — a dear friend, but he holds the oddest views and will engage all and sundry in his theories upon putting the world to rights." She paused before asking delicately, her eyes still on the work in her lap. "Did you happen to hear our conversation?"

"Only a very little," prevaricated the girl. "I think you were talking about gardening — didn't you mention white r-roses?"

The older woman laughed deprecatingly.

"My hobby, again, I'm afraid. Poor Sir John, finds it very boring, I know, and hardly pretends to listen to me."

Returning to her sewing, she made a little shooing gesture to Anna. "Run along and see if my niece has recovered from her bad temper," she said, selecting a thread from the colourful tangle in her work box.

Angry noises from a clavichord were echoing through the house, so Anna had no difficulty in tracing the Irish girl to the music room, where she was sitting in front of the instrument, striking the keyboard with stiff fingers, her back expressive of her feelings.

Anna watched for a moment, amused to hear Bach played as he never intended, before she spoke.

"I am sure you express your feelings perfectly, but if you are not careful you will break a nail and ruin the look of your hands for a week or more."

The music stopped abruptly and discordantly as Cecilia crashed her hands down on the ivory notes.

"I do believe you're right," she wailed, examining her fingers closely. "Two! and all the fault of that wretched brother of mine!"

A hastily smothered laugh broke from Anna and the other girl looked up quickly.

"Are you laughing at me?" she demanded haughtily, her eyebrows nearly meeting in a scowl.

Pointing out that she found the fact of the absent James being blamed for two broken finger nails amusing, Anna went on to suggest pacifically that Ensign Weston would most probably prove a more attentive and interesting escort than a near relation.

Observing the truth of this, Cecilia added darkly that she only hoped Jason was not already engaged and encouraged by the older girl, allowed herself to be persuaded to sit down and pen a persuasive note to the soldier.

While they awaited his reply, Anna set out to distract Cecilia, and recollecting the purchases of the morning soon had her examining her new possessions and refurbishing her already extensive wardrobe.

"Lord knows why I brought these

gowns from Ireland — I vow I hate them all," she sighed, eyeing disparagingly the silks and satins she had heaped upon her bed.

She held a striped silk against herself and eyed her reflection in the mirror. "Whatever persuaded me that I could wear mauve?" she wondered.

Anna examined the sweetpea coloured silk against the shining blonde curls and had to agree that it was not really the most flattering colour.

"You have it," said Cecilia, impulsively, tossing it towards her. "It'll suit you and no-one will recognise it, for I've not worn it here."

Unable to resist glancing in the mirror, Anna saw that the soft colour brought out her own dark hair and eyes, but felt she had to demur at taking so costly a gift.

Cessy smiled. "It suits you much better than it ever did me," she said honestly, adding ruefully that such a thing often happened. Seeing the other still hesitating, she patted her arm and said. "Please take it — it would give me pleasure to give you a present."

Anna smiled in return and accepted

the gift gracefully. "H-how kind you are, but you must let me do something in return — I'm very good with my needle, perhaps I can sew for you?"

"La, Betty would go into a fit of the sulks and never come out of them, if I suggested such a thing!" exclaimed Cecilia. "But she would allow you to trim a hat or two for me — something I'll confess, I dislike. Somehow it never comes out as I've intended."

Anna had no false modesty about her own nimble fingers and urging the other to bring out her hats and trimmings, set about her self-imposed task.

Ensign Weston declaring himself delighted to escort them both to the musical party, the girls were ready and waiting for him in the small parlour when he presented himself the next evening. Anna was almost sure that Ben Bow was one of the Link boys waiting by the two sedan-chairs in the dark street, but the flaring torches cast such black, dancing shadows that she could not be certain.

Lord and Lady Pakenham were awaiting their guests in the large hall of their house and greeted Anna with as much warmth as if they had known her for years instead of being introduced for the first time.

"There, I told you they were the nicest couple and that you need have no fear," whispered Cecilia as they walked into the ballroom where the concert was to be given.

"I feel I am here on false pretences — how can they have invited me?"

Cecilia gave her light laugh. "Because I wrote and asked them to, goose," she murmured.

Elegant, gilt chairs were arranged round the room in a circle and in the middle a group of musicians were already seated beside a harpsichord. The first piece they played was the one that Cecilia had so mistreated the day before and Anna could not resist stealing a quick glance in her direction. Meeting eyes that were brimful of suppressed mirth, she looked away hastily before she should lose her composure and tried to concentrate on the music.

Half expecting to find Captain Bellamy among the audience, she allowed her eyes to wander over the occupants of the room, until certain that he was not in their number, she relaxed and prepared to enjoy the evening.

Jason Weston proved the most attentive of escorts, divided his attentions equally between his charges, and when a cold supper was served, performing prodigiously in seeing that both ladies were happy.

"You really are the kindest fellow," Cecilia told him as he seated himself between them, having presented them both with filled plates and wine glasses.

Anna was surprised to see a faint flush rise in his cheeks at the Irish girl's praise and glanced quickly across at her, only to find that Cecilia had already lost interest in her escort and was busily examining the occupants of the room.

Catching the young soldier's eyes, Anna read all too clearly the emotion in their depths and looked away quickly before he should become aware of her own understanding of his feelings.

"D-do you care for Bach's music, Mr Weston?" she asked hastily, snatching at the first subject that presented itself to her mind.

He hesitated before glancing at her conspiratorially, he bent his head towards her and whispered. "To tell the truth, Miss Stanton, I have no great care for this kind of music. Give me a good rousing chorus and a sweet tune that I know and I'll be happy, but to my mind there's nothing like the fifes and drums that set us soldiers amarching."

"Then how noble to accompany us tonight," she exclaimed, much struck by his kindness.

"No such thing," he said, looking a little uncomfortable. "I count myself fortunate to play escort to two such delightful ladies."

Cecilia had picked disinterestedly at her plate and now was impatient to move. "Pray let us circulate," she said, standing up, her voluminous hoops swaying. "I vow the people I would speak with are without end — I will introduce you to all the people I know, Anna, and then you will be included in all the invitations."

Now that she was aware of his regard for Cecilia, Anna could see Jason Weston's attachment displayed in many ways she had not noticed before; how attentive he was to any wants of the Irish girl, and how quick to sense her needs and how eager to do her service. She also could not but notice how unaware of his feelings Cecilia was, accepting all his attentions with unnoticing indifference, as her due.

However even her sympathy for the love lorn soldier could not keep her awake that night. Unused to the late hours kept in Essex Street, Anna fell asleep almost as soon as she climbed into bed, only to be awakened out of a deep sleep, by the sounds of arrival from downstairs. For a moment she lay listening to the murmur of voices and soft movement, until the house grew quiet again and unsure whether she had been dreaming, she drifted back to sleep.

Meeting James Drelincourt on the stairs next morning proved that she had not dreamed the happenings of the night and she greeted him with a smile.

"I thought I heard someone in the night," she said, pausing, one hand on the banisters.

Looking up to where she stood above him, he smiled and sketched a quick bow. "Did I disturb you? My apologies for making so much noise."

"I am a light sleeper," she told him. "I am glad that you are back safely."

"Safely? You make it sound as if I rode to the ends of the earth. I only went to Oxford."

"Any journey can be dangerous," she pointed out gravely.

"I am a good horseman and fear no highwayman." He climbed the few stairs between them until he was beside her. "Were you worried about me?" he asked teasingly.

"Your sister was," Anna answered dampeningly.

He came nearer. "Confess, Miss Anna, that you were, too."

Her eyes flew to his face, flushing slightly at what she found there. "A — little," she agreed, looking away.

"Then, if I've made you miss me, my journey was worthwhile," he declared, and possessing himself of her hand dropped a light kiss on her fingers, before passing on up the stairs, leaving Anna with a strangely fluttering heart.

No-one she had encountered in the little town of Alstead had prepared her for such a man as James Drelincourt.

Suspecting that he flirted with every woman he met, Anna found herself hoping against all commonsense that he did not.

The young Irishman filled much of her thoughts that day and, when later, she heard his voice in the small parlour and the door was half open, she entered without thinking and with only the lightest of taps against the panelling to announce her entrance.

For a moment the people in the room were still as in a tableau, then Cecilia turned to her with a smile of welcome, Lady Primrose seated herself calmly and James dropped something into his aunt's workbox. It all happened in the second she paused on the threshold and was over quickly, leaving her to wonder if she had imagined the incident.

"Miss Anna, you don't know how pleased I am to see you," cried James, coming forward to take her hand and lead her into the room. "Cessy is just scolding me for forgetting my promise and riding away to Guildford."

Anna looked up, her steps faltering as she crossed the polished floor. "Guildford?

I thought you said Oxford when we met on the stairs."

Frowning slightly James shook his head. "That would have been rather out of my way — my friends live in Guildford."

"Perhaps I misheard you," said Anna, non-committally, but privately wondering at the inconsistency, the incident only serving to make her more curious about the object James had secreted among Lady Primrose's silks and needles.

Determined to find out what it was she waited until Lady Primrose was in her room, dressing to go out and then, certain that the room was empty, made an excuse of a lost handkerchief and returned there, pushing the door to behind her.

It was the work of moments to plunge her hand in among the tangled threads, feeling for whatever had been hidden there. Her fingers encountered a small, round object and bringing it out, she found it was a metal medallion of some kind. Examining it closer, she saw a head of a young man on one side and a withered tree with one newly sprouting branch on the other. She just had time to make out the word Revirescit when a noise in the hall warned her of danger and she hastily dropped the medal back into the workbox and looked up to find James Drelincourt standing in the doorway, regarding her with an unfathomable expression.

"Cessy sent me to help you find your handkerchief," he said impassively.

"Yes — h-how stupid of me to have dropped it," said Anna, wondering if he had seen her action. "I know I had it when we were here earlier."

"Let me help." Coming into the centre of the room, he gazed slowly around and Anna was glad that she had had the forethought to place her handkerchief in an appropriate position before she searched the workbox. "Here it is," he said, bending to retrieve the square of linen and lace from under a chair.

"How kind you are," smiled the girl. "I cannot think why I couldn't find it myself." From James' expression he was wondering the same thing and she hastened to give him an explanation that would relieve his suspicions. "To tell you the truth, I was just about to look in

110

Lady Primrose's box," she confided.

James' eyes narrowed and the look he turned on her was suddenly keen.

"I noticed that your aunt is almost out of blue silk and thought I could get her some more as a little surprise . . . she has been so kind to me, you see. I should like to please her. I thought if I snipped off a small piece, I could be certain to match it."

"I see." His relief was obvious and his tone much more friendly. "Let me help you."

Crossing quickly to the box, he reached in and took out a bundle of silks, handing them to his companion, while one hand went to the pocket in the voluminous skirts of his coat. If she had not been watching for such a move Anna would have been unaware of his action, but as it was she was certain that the medallion had been removed to a safer place.

Anna climbed the stairs to her room with knees grown strangely weak; for the first time she had realised that the situation in which she found herself was real. The tangible evidence of the Jacobite medal had blown away any feelings of unreality or play-acting she might have had and suddenly she was conscious not only of danger, but of guilt and unhappiness at spying on people who had shown her so much kindness.

She was seated in the deep windowsill staring blankly out at the garden when a quick scratch at the door announced Cecilia's entrance.

"Aunt Anne wants me to visit my Godmother tomorrow," she announced without preamble. "She's ancient and lies abed all day — really too old to see anyone, which means I ask you to accompany me."

Anna smiled. "Remember I am your companion," she reminded the other. "I do what you want — you don't have to entertain me, you know. Besides I have something to do and that will be just the opportunity I need."

Cecilia's face cleared. "The silks for my aunt, you mean. James told me about your idea." She gave Anna an impulsive hug. "What a dear girl you are to be sure," she said, her brogue very much in evidence, totally unaware of the effect her words had upon the other.

Concealing her feelings as best she could, Anna smiled and talked her way through the rest of the day, every word and incident of kindness from the Drelincourt family causing her painful pangs of guilt, until she longed to confess her duplicity.

Rising weary and heavy eyed after a sleepless night, she wished desperately that she had never met Rafe Bellamy, that she and Kit had not left the safe haven of their vicarage home ... but then, she was forced to admit, she would not have met James Drelincourt and that was something about which she had not the slightest regret.

5

CECILIA and Lady Primrose set off on their call the next afternoon, leaving Anna to go in search of Cecilia's maid, however that young lady proving impossible to find, she decided not to wait for someone to accompany her, but set off alone as she would have done had she still been living at Green Square.

Her purchase was soon made and wondering if James would make it his business to notice if she really had supplied his aunt with new sewing silk, she left the shop and began walking along the Strand towards Essex Street.

She had not gone far on her way, when a sibilant hissing drew her attention to a narrow side alley, and peering between the tall houses, she could just make the beckoning figure of Ben Bow.

"Miss, miss. Over here, miss."

"What do you want?" she asked, intrigued.

Shaking his head, he beckoned impatiently and Anna took a wary footstep towards him. Glancing over his shoulder, the boy ran ahead of her down the dim alley, while the girl hesitated in the entrance. Something in the child's manner gave the impression of urgency and against her better judgment she followed him along the uneven cobblestones, in time to see him slip past a decrepit black coach that almost blocked the other end of the alley.

Preparing to slide past as the boy had done, she was stopped by the ancient door swinging open and a hand reaching out towards her. Before she could move or call out, her arm was seized and she was pulled into the coach, while the horses were whipped up and the vehicle moved forward with unexpected speed.

Gasping with fright, she turned to her molester and saw a familiar pair of eyes watching her.

"Did you think you were being abducted?" Captain Bellamy asked lazily, leaning back against the cracked leather of the seat.

Anna, who had thought precisely that,

glared at him and tried to smooth her ruffled feelings, realising now that there had been something familiar about the appearance of the ancient vehicle.

"I suppose you own this — " she glanced round, showing her distaste for the dingy seat and dusty windows, "this *equipage*, for surely it was this vehicle that nearly ran me over the other day?"

Smiling, he bowed his head slightly. "The very same," he agreed. "How observant of you to notice."

"There could hardly be two — "

"On the contrary, there are many — so many that no-one will notice this, or remember having seen it."

Settling her wide-brimmed hat, Anna clasped her hands in her lap and gazed out of the window. "Where are you taking me?" she asked, watching the tall, narrow houses and realising with sudden unease that they were in a part of London that she had never seen. The streets were narrow and uneven and the windows of the houses, broken and dirty. When she caught glimpses of their occupants, they appeared coarse and unkempt, staring at the coach with sullen eyes.

"Best keep out of sight," advised her companion. "The people hereabouts have no liking for the gentry, or anyone better dressed than they."

Shrinking back in her corner, she stared at him. "W-where are you taking me?" she asked again.

"Merely for a ride," he told her kindly. "I thought we could talk without fear of interruption or being seen." Waiting for her to speak, the silence in the coach grew almost tangible and at last he asked impatiently what she had to tell him.

"N-nothing," she answered, her stutter more in evidence than usual.

The silence between them grew while she studied her gloves and smoothed the material of her skirts, refusing to lift her eyes and meet his gaze. After a while the silence became unbearable and she stole a glance at him from under her lashes, only to have his grey eyes seize upon hers and hold them. With a lift of his eyebrows he interrogated her and she swallowed miserably.

"I know that James has been away," he said. "I can imagine upon what errand, but I would like you to confirm my suspicions."

"He says he went to Guildford."

His smile did not reach his eyes, which remained cold and clear as ice. "Ah, but we know better than that, don't we, Miss Anna?"

Anna hung her head and smoothed her skirt with one finger. "I believe — I *think* he might have gone to Oxford," she said carefully.

"Now why should you suppose such a thing?" he wondered gently.

"I h-heard talk about a Dr King, who is something in one of the colleges there."

"Principal of St Mary's," Rafe Bellamy supplied kindly.

"Tell me what you have heard about our voluble Dr King."

"Not a great deal — merely that he made a — a speech — "

"A *Jacobite* speech," clarified the man opposite.

"If you know, why do you ask me?" Anna wanted to know, crossly.

"I am perfectly aware of Dr King's actions. I want to know how many others are as well informed as I — or as interested. Pray continue."

"That's all, really . . . save that there was some talk of the white rose becoming suddenly wealthy."

His eyebrows rose. "Elucidate," he commanded briefly and Anna's eyes fell under his gaze.

"There were a great many people around, all talking . . . it was very difficult to hear and yet not appear to be listening."

"What did you hear?"

"Th-that a lot of money had been deposited with a banker in Paris," she said, hoping that he would be satisfied with the information she had given him.

Captain Bellamy seemed amused. "Their espionage is almost as good as ours," he remarked to himself, before he fell to silently studying the girl before him.

Anna moved uneasily under his scrutiny.

"May I go now?" she asked. "I'll be missed soon and if I'm away too long, I shall have difficulty in explaining my absence."

"No doubt you'll think of something."

Anna endured his gaze a little longer,

doing her best to appear calm and indifferent, while her hands grew clammy and her heart beat quickened. "Then pray ask the driver to return to the Strand," she said, a hint of impatience hiding the unease in her voice.

"When you have told me all."

Her eyes flew to his face. "There's nothing m-more to tell," she said quickly, unhappily aware of the betraying stutter.

Stretching his long legs as best he could in the cramped space between the long seats, he flicked a speck of dust from the knee of his green velvet breeches. "My dear Anna, you must be aware that you have a slight hesitation in your speech which most people find delightful — I find it useful as well as attractive for it appears without fail whenever you are nervous or agitated. I own to finding this journey as tedious as you — but here we'll stay until you have told me why Mr Drelincourt went to Oxford."

Anna swallowed miserably and worried her lip. "I don't know why he went to Oxford," she said slowly, hoping to convince the man opposite of the truth of her statement, "but I do know he brought back a medallion which he showed to Lady Primrose and Cessy and hid from me."

"Did you see it?"

She nodded. "He hid it in Lady Primrose's workbox and I went back later on pretext of having mislaid my handkerchief. It had a head on one side and on the other a dead tree with one live branch and the word 'Revirescit'."

"I have seen it," he said gravely, and seemed to be considering her, apparently noticing for the first time her air of nervousness. "Do I afright you?" he asked suddenly. "Or are you afraid of something else?"

"I — think James suspects me."

"How so?"

"W-when I took the medallion I found him in the doorway, watching me. I wasn't sure if he'd seen anything and made an excuse to be looking in the workbox, but I don't know if he believed me."

Captain Bellamy considered, pursing his lips slightly. "All good intriguers are careful," he stated. "Drelincourt has to be cautious and you are a new, and virtually unknown, member of his household."

"But they seem so careless — talking about Charles Edward Stuart almost openly the other night. Others could have listened as well as I."

"To some, the Jacobite cause is almost a game, a little ploy to pass the time. *They* are the ones you'll hear talking, but to James Drelincourt and others as fanatical as he, it is their mission in life to restore the Stuarts to the throne of England. They are the dangerous ones. The others we can dismiss, but James and his ilk are serious men and it is to them that I want you to listen. Do you understand?"

"Yes. Lady Primrose and her friends will talk and plan and do nothing — "

His eyes narrowed. "I am not sure that we should include Lady Primrose among the nonentities. I believe she is cleverer and more astute than she appears. She doesn't hide that she is a Jacobite, indeed she rather parades the fact . . . as though wishing us all to know and laugh at her politics, and think her a silly, romantic woman." Reaching upwards, he rapped sharply on the coach side with his knuckles.

Considering this new aspect of Anne Primrose, Anna recalled that on a few occasions she had been aware of James bowing to his aunt's quietly expressed wishes and wondered if Rafe Bellamy could be right in his suppositions. Looking out of the dull window, she suddenly caught a glimpse of a busy thoroughfare and recognised the street through which they were passing.

Captain Bellamy put a detaining hand on her arm. "Watch for anything unusual, strangers arriving, surreptitious conversations — above all listen and try to find out if James has any papers. Take notice of any letters that arrive for him — or Lady Primrose."

A quiet whistle sounded from the driver and Rafe Bellamy released her arm. "The street is clear," he said and opened the narrow door for her. "Ben Bow will take any message for me," he added as the door swung to behind her.

The coachman gathered up his reins and the clumsy vehicle lumbered out of sight, leaving Anna alone in the empty alley.

"I'll walk home with you, miss," said a hoarse voice and Ben Bow appeared at her side. "The Cap'n says to look after you."

Anna looked at him curiously as they turned into the Strand. "Do you work for Captain Bellamy?"

"Yes, miss," she was told proudly. "I'm his runner, but just now I'm to watch out for you. If you ever wants me, I'll be around."

Digesting this, Anna walked on in silence for a while. "It's a great pity that he does not pay you better," she remarked at last, having taken in her companion's clothing. "At least he could buy you a new suit."

"Lor' love you!" exclaimed the boy, smoothing his torn and grubby sleeve. "It's my disguise — no-one notices a street boy. I might as well not be here for all the notice folk take of me."

Anna was uncertain, but a little later, she had to agree with him; having reached Essex Street, he slipped from her side, and, mingling with the passersby, was lost to her view almost before she was aware of his absence. Later that night when she paused on the landing on her way to bed and saw a small familiar figure, curled up in the doorway opposite, she was strangely comforted, feeling more secure at the presence of one known friend.

So busy was Anna and so involved in the Drelincourt family that several weeks had slipped by, before she realised that it had been some time since she had heard from Kit. Filled with remorse at her neglect, she hurriedly penned him a letter and so was not altogether surprised when Betty announced a few days later that a visitor awaited her in the morning room.

"Kit!" she cried joyfully as the slim soldier turned from the window and she recognised her brother despite the severe white wig framing his youthful face.

For a moment she hugged him unreservedly while he patted her shoulder, before putting him away from her, she admired his uniform and manner, noting with pleased surprise how he seemed to have matured in the short while since she had seen him.

"How smart and brave you are," she exclaimed. "I vow I hardly knew my soldier brother." Slipping her arm through his she led him across the room to a tall sash-window that was open onto the terrace. "Let us go into the garden," she suggested and they stepped over the low windowsill.

With arms linked they were content to stroll over the lawn and exchange news. Anna was delighted at Kit's obvious enjoyment of the army life and listened enthralled to his tales and anecdotes.

"Tell me," she said at last, drawing him down onto a seat beneath the shade of a spreading tree, "did they let you come because I was worried?"

Her brother gave a shout of laughter, that startled her and frightened away several birds.

"Dear Sis, what an idea!" Kit spluttered. "Fond as I am of you, the regiment would look for another reason before giving me furlough. I'm here to have another uniform fitted."

"I see," she murmured, a little chagrined, before asking in sudden alarm. "You're not going abroad are you? Jason Weston

126

is going to the Americas and try as I will, I couldn't like the idea if you were to be sent there."

"Have no fear — we're to be stationed in England as far as I know."

As Anna sighed with relief, Cecilia joined them, pausing on the path to smile and give Kit her hand.

"How pleased I am to see you," she said frankly. "Poor Anna was quite worried — I daresay you are very busy, but I think it too bad of you not to have written to her."

She laughed as the young soldier apologised contritely and declared that she would set her brain to devising a suitable punishment. "To be sure I have the very thing," she said suddenly. "Aunt Anne is giving a soirée tomorrow. The dullest thing, I can tell you, but if you contrive to come and enliven us, Anna and I shall forgive you. Will you still be in London, or must you haste away back to your regiment?"

"I believe they can manage without me," Kit told her. "At least I am not expected back for a few days." He bowed solemnly and kissed the Irish girl's hand formally. "Thank you for your invitation — I shall be delighted to come."

Anna hid a smile at the air of elegance he assumed, thinking privately how dashing he looked in his red and gold uniform; her heart filling with sisterly pride, as she saw that Cecilia made no attempt to hide the fact that she found him interesting.

However she was unable to restrain a glow of family pride, when the next evening, she caught sight of her brother among the throng of guests, in the full glory of his new uniform. Ensign Weston was also among the party and the two soldiers in their regimentals brought a particularly masculine impact to the gaily dressed guests.

"Sure and they fill all the other men with envy," a voice whispered wickedly in her ear and Anna turned to find Cecilia at her elbow.

"Was I so transparent?" she asked ruefully.

"Well — I wasn't altogether sure which military man you were looking at," teased her friend, "but there is something especial about a uniform. I must confess to being a little bored with these London fops — I don't really care for men in pale satins and with patches on their faces. I don't like a man to look like a be-breeched version of myself!"

Anna laughed. "You are unkind, Cessy," she protested. "Not all the men look effeminate. No-one could accuse your brother of not looking masculine."

"No — but then he's James and a rule to himself. I don't believe he cares a fig for fashion, but he always contrives to look right. Now myself . . . I'm never sure if I'm right, somehow I'm either too bright or downright dowdy. You remember I bought the orange ornament to wear with my green gown, but when I put it on tonight I could see at once that it wouldn't do."

"It will look very nice with your cream brocade," Anna offered placatingly.

"And Aunt Anne said I made a vulgar display with my jewelry and made me take off a bracelet and a brooch."

"You'll be able to wear it when you're older," Anna consoled her. "At the moment you have no need of diamond adornment."

Cecilia looked at her, before dimpling in pleasure. "You say the nicest things, Anna dear," she cooed and patted her arm before sailing away on an aura of satisfaction.

"Are you to entertain us Miss Stanton?" enquired Ensign Weston who had joined her, nodding towards the group round the harpsichord which had been brought down from the music room for the occasion.

"I'm afraid I don't play well enough to perform in public, but Lady Primrose has persuaded me to sing some country airs later."

The soldier grimaced ruefully. "Lady Primrose is a very persuasive person," he admitted. "Kit and I were committed to a round almost before we knew it."

"I'm sure you'll do it very well."

He made an expansive gesture with both hands. "I've hardly sung since I left the nursery."

"More's the pity you chose the profession you did — if you had been a Naval man, a sea-shanty or two would have dropped easily from your lips," Anna teased.

"Oh, I can shout a soldier song with

the best of 'em, but they would be hardly the thing for society company or delicate ears!"

Anna smiled at her brother as he came up and asked what round he proposed to sing.

"London's burning," he answered promptly. "It's the only one I know."

Admitting to herself that she doubted if her voice would stand up to the fine society in which she found herself, Anna waited her turn to perform with some trepidation, but when Cecilia played the opening bars and she lifted her voice in the well-known notes, her fears left her and she sang easily, pleasing the audience with her naturalness.

"Well done, Ann," Kit whispered in her ear as she left the harpsichord, and by the use of his childhood name for her, she knew that his praise was sincere.

Pausing near the large double doors to listen to the soldiers' rendering of the round, she noticed a stranger hovering in the shadows of the hall and thinking he must be a late guest, looked about to summon a footman to go to his assistance. Unable to find a servant within hailing distance, she looked again at the newcomer, wondering if she should go to his aid herself, when she was struck by something odd, almost furtive in his manner.

A voluminous black cloak wrapped him from chin to foot in its enveloping folds and a deep tricorn was pulled so low as to hide his face from view; the very way he stood back in the shadows and his still, yet alert, stance told her that here was no ordinary guest and a shiver of excitement slid down her spine.

Even as she watched a footman appeared and bent to whisper in the stranger's ear. The man nodded and lifted his head, giving Anna a glimpse of a sharp chin and thin features as he crossed the hall in the wake of the footman and was shown into the library at the back of the house.

Trying to hide her interest, Anna turned away, ostensibly viewing the guests and room before her, with the mild enjoyment expected at a soirée, but now that her attention had been aroused, she was alert and watchful for any untoward incident, and when a few moments later, James Drelincourt made an unobtrusive exit, she was not surprised.

Taking a glass of champagne from a nearby tray, she retired to a seat from which she could watch the door and waited with a growing sense of anticipation for James' return. However, when he did so, he appeared so free of mind, mixing with his friends and acquaintances with so much ease of manner and such little appearance of one bothered with thoughts of rebellion, that she began to doubt her own suppositions.

Supper was announced and the throng trooped into the dining room to partake of the cold collation laid there, with a thoughtful Anna trailing in their wake. She found herself in the midst of a group of young people, was supplied with a plate of delicacies and joined in the fun, responding to the pleasantries with a droll dryness that made her companions laugh, but all the while half her attention was given to James. Sometime later, she realised that he was circulating more quickly than was warranted and she did her best to keep him unobtrusively under observation as he paused and spoke a few words to various men, before moving on. To anyone watching it would have appeared nothing more than a host's good manners, but Anna felt she could detect a purposefulness in his manner that sent a tingle of anticipation down her back and her hands grew damp with something very like fear.

The food in her mouth turned to sawdust and she looked down at her plate with distaste.

"Let me fetch you a glass of wine — or some dessert. I fear that that which you have is not to your liking."

Looking up quickly Anna found James beside her and started so suddenly that but for his quick action, she would have dropped her plate.

"Did I frighten you?" he asked, concerned.

"I — was thinking," she told him hastily.

"You looked very serious. Surely nothing in my aunt's soirée can have caused the frown I saw."

Anna gazed at him blankly, trying to find an explanation he would accept for her preoccupation. "I was wondering if I was right in choosing pink ribbons for this gown — or if yellow would have set it off the better."

He appeared willing to give his attention to the matter and she knew that he had accepted her explanation as a female foible and suddenly she was exasperated by his obvious belief that women were incapable of any intelligent thought. Hiding her feelings as best she could, she replied to his opinions, entering into a mild flirtation until she was in a good temper again and could admit that the charm of his manner quite made up for his underestimation of the weaker sex.

Determined to watch for any other mysterious strangers or happenings, Anna hovered in the hall as the guests retired in desultory groups to the larger room, trying to be unobtrusive and yet look purposeful enough to quench anyone's wonder at her being there, but her presence at last caused a query and from one whom she would have preferred not to have noticed her hesitation in the hall.

"Why are you waiting here?" asked

Cecilia. "Come into the with-drawing room. I am going to persuade Jason and your brother to make up numbers in a group to sing madrigals."

Anna stared at her, seeking for a reasonable excuse. "I've t-torn my petticoat. I was just trying to slip upstairs without anyone noticing," she said at last, chiding herself unhappily for the growing ease with which the lie slid from her tongue.

The Irish girl gave her a little push in the direction of the stairs. "Off you go, then, Betty is waiting in my chamber for just such an event. Don't be long, though, I'll need you to take a part in the singing."

Anna hurried upstairs, pausing long enough on the landing to put her toe through the lace frill on her petticoat, hating her own duplicity, but knowing that Cecilia might learn of the lack of her visit to Betty if she did not pay a call on the waiting maid.

Much later when the soirée was over and the guests taking their leave, she was standing a little behind Lady Primrose and Cecilia as they bid their friends goodnight, when she became aware that certain of the guests were not leaving; occasionally, instead of murmuring pleasantries to their host and crossing the hall to the front door and waiting footmen, one would slip silently behind the milling, gossiping throng, along the short passage leading to the back of the house and the garden and into the Library.

Her pulses quickening with excitement, Anna told herself that there was no reason to suspect anything other than a late night card game, but knew in reality that the secrecy of their manner confirmed her already aroused suspicions.

Kit made an elegant leg to his hostess, before bidding his sister an affectionate farewell.

"I'll see you again?" she asked anxiously, unwilling to lose him again so soon.

He smiled and shook his head. "I must join my regiment tomorrow," he said, looking at her closely. "What's wrong, Ann — is something bothering you?"

Aware of the nearness of Cecilia and her aunt, Anna shook her head. "N-no — nothing. I miss you, Kit."

Ignoring the startled gazes of the remaining guests, he swept her into a brotherly hug. "I'll write," he promised, mistaking the cause of her unease. "Really, I will. My word upon it."

Giving a somewhat shaky laugh, Anna pulled his head down to hers and planted a kiss on his cheek. "Mind you do," she admonished. "I've witnesses to your promise!" and watched, still smiling, as Kit crossed the hall, pausing in the open doorway to flourish his cocked hat at her, before vanishing into the dark night outside.

The ladies retired to their chambers, leaving the servants to the task of removing the evidence of the evening's entertainment and soon the house grew still as its inmates made ready for bed.

In her chamber, Anna sat before her dressing-table, straining her ears for sounds from below. When all had been silent for some time, she knew she could delay no longer and reluctantly she stood up, taking a dark cloak from a wall cupboard.

Creeping down the stairs she became aware of the various noises in the sleeping house, where before all had seemed silent, now she could hear the loud ticking of a grandfather clock on the landing, gentle breathing whispered from Cecilia's room and to her dismay, each step of the stairs seemed to protest at her passing. Carefully, cautiously, her heart beating uncomfortably fast, she stole along the passage that led to the garden and now she could hear the soft murmur of men's voices. Drawing near to the Library, she could see a crack of light that spread out from under the door, crossing the floor and leaning her ear against the panelling she found she could make out words spoken within the room.

"No, no," said someone testily and Anna thought she recognised Sir John Sligh's voice. "It will all come to naught, you'll see."

James' clear tones rose above a murmur of protests. "You are too easily discouraged," he said not bothering to hide the scorn he felt. "Or — could it be that your feet grow cold?"

Sir John protested angrily, his vehemence sounding too loud and forced. "Monsieur brings us word that the Prince has ordered an agent in Antwerp to purchase muskets and other weapons. Do we need more proof, gentlemen, that His Highness is in earnest?"

His voice rose in excitement, the words carrying clearly to the listening girl, but obviously warned to greater caution his next words were quieter and she had to strain her ears to hear.

"Do I need to say, gentlemen, that I believe we may expect a visitor in the near future?"

A murmur of excitement broke from his listeners, masking his voice and when next Anna could hear clearly, James seemed to be asking his companions to commit themselves to support the Jacobite cause.

"We must be sure of our — friends," he was saying, "and so I must ask for a show of hands of all those willing to support the true King, either in presence, money or like. I promise that only His Highness will ever see the list beside myself."

There was a pause while Anna could imagine him looking round the room and then a murmured 'thank you, gentlemen' in a non-committal voice that spoke of neither satisfaction or disquiet.

Suddenly aware from noises within the room that the meeting was about to end, Anna drew back, half turning to run back to the hall, but realising that she would not have time to reach the stairs, instead raced to the garden door, dragged back the bolt with shaking hands, and let herself out into the damp night, just as the Library door opened, spilling golden candlelight into the dark passage behind her.

Running across the terrace and down the shallow steps to the garden she hurried along the gravel path, acutely aware of the noise made by each footfall and hid behind a large, spreading bush, her heart beating unevenly. Some minutes elapsed while her breathing returned to normal and she became aware of the heady perfume from the garden flowers on the still night air, before she dared to move and peer round her leafy refuge; the house appeared to be in darkness and with a sigh of relief, she stepped out from her hiding place.

Thinking it wiser to walk boldly, in

case anyone should be watching from the window, she made no attempt at secrecy, stepping out bravely and even daring to hum a little tune beneath her breath. A few paces and she realised how wise she had been to adopt such an attitude, for she was suddenly certain that she was not alone. Her foot faltered a little and her heart began to race against her tight bodice, but she managed to walk on with every appearance of calm.

"Has no-one told you that night air can be dangerous?" asked a voice suddenly and James stepped out from the shadows, his powdered hair contrasting strongly with the dark blue of his watered-silk coat.

Anna allowed herself a startled gasp. "M-Mr Drelincourt — how you frightened me!"

"My apologies," he said gravely, inclining his head. "It seems to be an unfortunate habit of mine." For a moment he looked down, seeming to be studying her, his bright eyes very clear and pale in the moonlight. "Now you are here, Miss Anna, will you do me the honour of taking a turn about the garden with me?"

"It's rather late — " she protested, unhappily aware of the impropriety of the action, but her demur was ignored and her hand drawn through the crook of his arm and firmly held there. Almost willy-nilly she found herself once more stepping down onto the path and walking towards the familiar bulk of the spreading shrub.

"Tell me," her companion said easily, "do you often take a midnight stroll?"

"Hardly ever," she answered readily.

"Then may one ask why you felt the need tonight?"

"I — couldn't sleep."

His gaze fell to the shape of her hoop swinging beneath the enveloping cloak and she hurried on. "I knew I could not, even before I went to my chamber. I was too excited — "

"Just so," he interposed smoothly. "I hope nothing disturbed you?"

"No, I told you. I felt restless and came down again."

Opening her eyes wide, she tried to look up at him. "Did I do wrong?"

she asked appealingly. "I heard your friends playing cards in the Library and supposed that as the household was not yet asleep no-one would object if I went out."

She felt rather than heard him catch his breath at mention of the unseen guests and did her best to hold his gaze, her own eyes as wide and candid as she could make them.

The grip on her fingers tightened; and then slowly relaxed as he scrutinised her upturned face and at last appeared satisfied with her innocence.

"My aunt would not approve," he said, leading her on towards the statue at the end of the path. "She holds that night air can be dangerous."

"So you mentioned before," Anna pointed out, ignoring the double meaning behind his words. Suddenly aware of his nearness, she drew away a little and suggested that they should return to the house.

"I had not suspected that you agreed with Lady Primrose," James commented dryly a hint of laughter in his voice.

Stung, Anna looked up. "You know

very well I have no fear of night chills," she cried indignantly and knew at once that she had made a mistake.

"Then, surely you are not afraid of *me*?" James possessed himself of her free hand and carried her fingers in turn to his lips.

Conscious of his nearness and masculinity, Anna caught her breath. "Sh-should I be?" she asked her voice shaking slightly with the sudden realisation of just how attractive she found him.

"That, my dear Anna, you'll have to answer for yourself."

James' voice was deep and quiet in the still garden. She thought he intended to kiss her as he tipped up her chin, in what was almost a caress but after a moment he released her, taking her arm again as he led her towards the sleeping house.

6

PONDERING on the ambiguity of James' conversation and shaken by the unexpected emotions he had aroused Anna slept badly, rising heavy eyed and threatened by a headache. Neither was her wretchedness lightened during the days that followed, for the Drelincourt family seemed to overwhelm her with kindness, Lady Primrose treating her with the affection of an absentminded aunt and Cessy with all the fondness of a long standing friendship . . . while James appeared to seek her out with an obvious preference for her company until she almost suspected him of paying court to her.

The days passed quickly and now the garden in Essex Street was a vivid mass of colourful blooms, their heavy scent drifting in through the open windows and filling the tall house with the perfume of summer.

Anna grew uneasy, knowing that she

should have reported the Jacobite meeting to Captain Bellamy, but with each day the act seemed more like betrayal and she could not bring herself to send a message, hoping that no news of the newly bought weapons would reach his ears and make him suspect her duplicity.

Cecilia and Lady Primrose busied themselves with plans for a supper party in Ranelagh Gardens.

"Just a little daring," confided Lady Primrose to Anna, "but with you there, I am sure there can be no question of impropriety — you're such a sensible person."

Anna was a little doubtful whether she could sustain such trust, but Cecilia persuaded her to accept the obligation.

"Pray don't say no," she pleaded. "Sure and it's the thing I've most wanted to do since arriving in London. Aunt Anne has been on the point of agreeing many times, but always a suitable excuse has presented itself . . . you know how she hates playing chaperon. I promise we'll all be good."

"You make me feel like a governess," protested Anna.

The Irish girl laughed. "Mine was over fifty and more interested in riding to hounds than educating me," she said. "You'll give us the guard of your presence, then?"

Against her better judgement, Anna nodded and when her agreement was made known to Lady Primrose that lady declared a wish to present both the young ladies with a new gown for the occasion.

"But you have given me enough already," cried Anna.

"And you, my dear Anna, have given me a great deal in return. Much as I enjoy having my niece to stay here with me, I will be the first to admit that I have no liking for playing the duenna." She shot Cessy a speaking glance and the Irish girl dimpled in return. "You save me much effort — and leave me precious time for other matters. It relieves my mind to know that Cessy is in good, capable hands," Lady Primrose went on to Anna, reaching across to pat her knee. "Now, no argument if you please. You and Cessy visit the mantua maker and have the bill presented to me. All I ask is that you both look your prettiest and enjoy yourselves."

After that the plans went ahead quickly, even James falling in with the proposal and offering to take arrangements for supper upon himself. Cecilia and Anna spent a happy afternoon in the dressmaker's establishment, closeted with pattern books and materials. With some difficulty, Anna weaned the younger girl's choice away from a length of fashionable mustard yellow silk and influenced her to select an ethereal almond green silk with a faint silver stripe, choosing herself, a white brocade, patterned with silver rosebuds.

"Will my orange feathers go with it?" Cecilia wondered later, retaining a straight face until she caught the other girl's appalled expression.

"Cessy!" exploded Anna. "Those feathers are becoming my 'Bête Noire.'"

"Well, do you know," confided Cecilia. "I'm not nearly so keen on them as I was. I begin to think I might give them to Betty."

"I should think she'd be grateful," Anna agreed vehemently.

James coming in at that moment, he

demanded to know the reason for their merriment and joined in the laughter when they explained.

"My dear Miss Anna," he exclaimed, "Cessy has trunks full of her mistakes . . . she has a penchant from the most unsuitable styles and colours."

"Oh how untrue," his sister cried from the heart. "Just because I'm not an old stick-in-the-mud who's afraid to wear any but the dullest of colours — !"

James turned to Anna, his arms flung wide in mock appeal. "I turn to you for justice — you shall be our Paris, even if you are of a different gender to that youth. How say you, Miss Anna, *am* I a conventional dullard?"

Looking from one bright, challenging face to the other, Anna hesitated, pondering her task. "To be sure the colours you choose are a trifle dark," she began doubtfully, "but are usually of such rich brilliance and suit you so well, I don't think they can be called dull."

"There, you see," he turned to his sister in triumph.

"But then," went on the other girl,

unperturbed by his interruption, "a little experimentation, something unexpected, unusual, can be relied upon to make life interesting."

Cecilia smiled and James turned to her, his interest caught.

"You should be a diplomat," he told her, "You leave us both pleased."

"It is part of my duty."

"Duty. Never speak of duty," cried Cessy. "You become more of a dear friend each day — more of a sister almost. What say you James?"

Anna looked up and found his bright gaze full upon her and something in his eye made her drop her glance hastily, while a warm blush rose to her cheeks.

"Never a sister," he answered slowly. "I would have no claim of blood relationship with our dear friend, here."

"Churlish, James?" wondered his sister, who had not seen his expression from where she stood.

Smiling, he shook his head and bent to possess himself of Anna's hand, carrying it to his lips with a courtly gesture. "I would not be a brother to you," he said softly, "as I believe you know."

Anna looked at him, lost for words, and made a helpless little gesture with her free hand. At once it was gathered close and imprisoned with its twin.

"Do I embarrass you?" he asked quietly. "Believe me I had no intention of that. This is not the time and place . . . but allow me to hope that I may express myself more clearly in the future — "

"What are you muttering about?" demanded his sister crossly. "It's very rude to talk in whispers, James."

At once he released Anna and swung round, saying easily, "How go the preparations for our al fresco supper? Are the invitations sent?"

"Of course," Cecilia was huffy, turning an irritated shoulder to him. "You have been so busy with making the supper arrangements, that you haven't considered how much we have done. The booth is booked, the carriages and seats arranged and the day set."

"I wish that a husband could be found for you, Cessy," her brother said pleasantly. "One that will take you far away and beat you regularly."

Forgetting the dignity of her years, the fair girl pulled a face at him and turned to her friend.

"You may wonder why we reside in London and yet never go to Court," she said deliberately provoking. "I do assure you it's not because we have been banned from such functions, or are not aristocratic enough to attend them."

"Cessy!"

Ignoring her brother she went on. "Neither is it because we can't afford the dress required, or because we cannot find a dowager willing to present me — James has his convictions and we all have to bow down to them. None of us may make our bow to a Hanoverian!"

"Cecilia!"

James' voice thundered across the room, stopping his sister with a gasp. One look at his face and even she knew she had gone too far. With a stifled sob, she stamped her foot at him and, snatching up her skirts in ungraceful bunches, ran from the room.

For a moment there was silence in the room, while the sounds of her retreating heels could be heard, then James sighed

153

deeply and crossed to close the door.

"Now you know," he said, leaning his shoulders against the panels. "If you have not suspected before."

"I — h-had wondered."

"Of course. Anyone of intelligence would and you, my dear Anna, are not I think in precisely the usual mould of female intellect."

"I am not sure what you mean by that," Anna said candidly, while her pulse quickened at thought of what the conversation ahead might reveal, "but if you mean that I must have suspected you are Jacobites, then, yes, I have — for some time. I didn't know that your aunt made any attempt to conceal it."

"We are really very incompetent," he remarked, watching her carefully.

"Does it matter?" she asked. "Surely, the need for secrecy would only arise if you were involved in restoring the Stuarts to the throne." She allowed herself a sad smile and went on wistfully. "Like most Tories, you long for the old days . . . toast the King over the water and wish him well — "

Leaving the door, he crossed the room

to her and, suddenly afraid to meet his eyes, Anna turned away to gaze unseeingly out of the long window. Hands took her shoulders and turned her to face him. Startled to find him so close, she involuntarily looked up and found her eyes imprisoned.

"And you, Anna — what of you?"

Trying to smile and speak lightly, she said, "I wear the white rose, you know."

"That could mean anything. I want to know your politics." He spoke almost harshly, his voice rough and the girl was suddenly afraid.

"Are women allowed politics?" she asked, tearing her eyes from his, with something approaching a physical effort.

Shaking her slightly, his grip almost a caress, with one finger under her chin, he turned up her face.

"Not many would be interested," he allowed. "But, I've a feeling that you are more intelligent than to concern yourself solely with frills and furbelows."

"This is a new view," she pointed out, "and one I had not suspected you of holding."

She felt a laugh shake him. "Until I met you, I had no idea that females were interested in anything other than lovers and fashions, but now — "

The door behind them opened with an audible rattle of the latch and as James released her, Anna turned to it with a rush of relief that she was saved, at least for the moment, from having to answer his question.

"James?" Lady Primrose spoke his name on a query, her voice low and worried, and her nephew crossed the room quickly to take her hands reassuringly.

"It's alright," he said. "She is aware of our beliefs and declares she is one of us."

Lady Primrose sighed and sat down on the chair beside her workbox. "You mean — ?"

"She is a good Tory," James put in quickly and to Anna's acute senses, there was a warning note in his voice, "and toasts the King over the water regularly. We need have no fear that she will run to the military with tales of our perfidy in wishing the old days were back again."

His aunt raised her pale eyes to his,

reading the message there, before she turned to the watching girl, and held out her hand.

"Come here, my dear," she said. "You have no idea what a relief it is, not to have to hide my politics from you any more. Not that we do more than remember the Stuarts and send money to make life more bearable for them in exile."

"I am afraid that I have never done more than listen to tales and feel indignant — "

They exchanged glances and smiled at her frankness.

"Very few do more," said Lady Primrose comfortably, settling back in her chair, her inevitable needlework between her busy fingers.

"My father said that the Scottish Adventure was the last effort the Stuarts would make, that after that defeat their will to succeed was broken."

Pale blue eyes stared at her across the gaily embroidered material. "Hardly the words of a fervent Jacobite," Lady Primrose said sharply.

James cleared his throat warningly.

"He was obviously a man of foresight," he put in quickly. "One who thought for himself, not just accepting others' views."

"He spoke his mind, certainly," agreed Anna.

"And was doubtless a man of great charm to have won the affections of my dear governess," said the older woman, having recovered from her momentary annoyance. She folded her sewing and standing up, took her nephew's arm. "Now, this conversation is becoming too deep for me. James, take me out into the garden. I want to see how my apricot trees are doing."

"Will you accompany us?" asked James, not so obvious in his desires as his aunt.

Anna shook her head and said she would seek out Cecilia, leaving the room with her mind in a turmoil at the varying emotions she seemed to have aroused in the others; while Lady Primrose appeared calm and placid almost to the point of dullness, Anna was beginning to suspect that a very different person dwelt behind the carefully maintained façade. And while James undoubtedly attracted her, her fascination was tempered at times by something akin to fear. Now and again she caught a glimpse of ruthlessness behind his charm that startled her into unease and she began to think unhappily that he would be as dangerous a man to cross as would Captain Bellamy.

Cecilia looked up quickly as the other girl entered and lifted her chin defiantly.

"Well?" she demanded, "are you going to betray us?"

Anna caught her breath sharply. "Wh-what makes you say that?"

The fair girl raised her eyebrows. "Now you know we hold Jacobite views," she explained.

"Oh that — I've known for ages," said Anna, with an attempt at ease, and crossed to the window.

"And *are* you going to send for the Military?"

"Of course not," Anna assured her, watching the foreshortened figures of Lady Primrose and her nephew in the garden below as they examined the trees growing in the sunshine against a sheltered wall. "James tells me that you are not acting Jacobites — but Tories like me." With an effort at frankness, she turned into the room and faced her friend. "I wish for the old days of Stuart Kings, but I don't think I would actually do much for them apart from declaring my loyalty, by passing my wine glass over water."

Cecilia smiled suddenly, her face clearing. "Exactly so," she declared, "how I feel precisely. The Stuarts are romantic and if the Prince had won five years ago . . . but now, I must confess to finding his cause the slightest bit boring." She giggled behind her hand. "Pray *don't* tell James. I've a feeling that he feels differently."

Silently Anna agreed with her, wondering if the other had an inkling of her brother's activities.

"And Lady Primrose?" she asked carelessly. "What does she think?"

"Aunt Anne?" repeated the Irish girl, consideringly. "She gives the impression of being interested in nothing but her needlework and garden . . . but sometimes I wonder. She seems pliable and easily led and yet suddenly, one can find her totally immovable. She's kind and generous and has been very good to us, but I sometimes think that we don't know Aunt Anne at all, that someone quite different lives behind her eyes and that she manages us all to her satisfaction."

Anna gazed at the other, surprised that Cecilia should have so much perception and voice her own feelings so exactly, but before she could speak, the fair girl smiled and shook herself.

"Let's talk about our Ranelagh party," she suggested. "How shall you do your hair? I think I might powder mine."

Falling in with her obvious desire, Anna fell to discussing the various merits of hairstyles and dressings, allowing that she herself, had never worn powder but owning to an eagerness to try the new fashion.

Consequently, when the day of the supper arrived the girls closeted themselves in Cecilia's chamber with Betty for several hours, emerging with white heads and a tendency to giggle.

James' eyes widened at the sight, but he had the good sense to make no remark apart from commenting upon the amount of worry he imagined they must have borne lately. Lady Primrose said roundly that it was a pity to hide the colour of their hair, but agreed, reluctantly, that the light powdering of white was becoming, and altogether rather pleased with the effect, the two girls accepted their escorts' arms and glided elegantly out to the waiting coach.

Cecilia and Anna were unable to suppress a gasp of delight as they drew up at the gates of Ranelagh as the dusk of evening fell and caught their first sight of the pleasure gardens. Tiny lights strung from tree to tree gave the impression of fairyland, shining on the people below as they strolled along the paths between the shrubs and booths, set like summer-houses among the lawns and statues. The rotunda was a blaze of lights and filled the girls with a longing to enter the circular building, but as it was a public night and open to all, they sensibly quelled their desires and looked forward eagerly to the quieter entertainment before them.

Eyes glittering with excitement from

behind their tiny, black 'loo' masks, they drew the folds of their dominoes around them and stepped down from the coach. James appeared to know the way and strode confidently along the dark paths. Whether by design or accident, Anna found herself on his arm, while Cecilia walked beside Ensign Weston.

The gardens were crowded with pleasure seekers and as a group of particularly boisterous youths dashed by, brushing against her wide hoop, Anna involuntarily shrank back against James. At once he drew her close to his side, tucking her under his arm, and looking back over his shoulder to see that Jason was caring for Cecilia in the same way.

"It's quieter by the boxes," he said, reassuringly. "There's no need to be frightened."

"I'm not frightened," Anna protested. "They startled me, that's all."

Amusement glinted through the eye-slits of his black mask. "Of course," he agreed, kindly and throwing his dark blue cloak back over his shoulders, led her along a path lined with open fronted booths.

"Well, to be sure this is quite delightful," exclaimed Cecilia looking round her new surroundings.

Examining the elegant table and chairs that furnished the box and the blaze of candles that lit it Anna had to agree with her. Going to the open front, she gazed out at the flickering fairy-lights that were strung across the path, linking each booth with the one opposite and stared, entranced at the boxes on either side of the path, each brilliantly lit with their occupants looking like actors upon a stage.

"Glad you agreed to play duenna to Cessy?" asked a voice by her elbow and she turned to find James so near that her shoulder brushed against the frills of his shirt front.

"Oh, yes, above all," she breathed. "It's beyond anything I expected. I would not be surprised if a fairy princess passed by, or a knight in armour appeared."

James laughed. "I'm afraid you'll have to make do with me," he said, his teeth gleaming against his tanned skin.

Anna caught her breath and hastily looked away, hoping that James had not read her startled gaze; to say at that moment that he appeared the image of Prince Charming himself would have been an understatement. With the candlelight and shadow contrasting across his high cheek bones, his silk cloak shimmering around his shoulders like a magic garment and his bright blue eyes smiling intimately down at her, he was the embodiment of every female's secret dream.

The door behind them opened, breaking the spell that held her with a rush of noise and greetings. With something approaching relief she turned to greet the arriving guests, hoping no-one would notice her flushed cheeks, or the pulse beating furiously in her throat.

Soon efficient servants entered with the supper and proceeded to set the table quietly. Anna's eyes widened as she seated herself and she wondered how so many delicacies could be produced so far from a kitchen.

"Champagne," said James, pouring the effervescent liquid into her glass. His eyes fell meaningly to the spray of white roses that she had pinned at the last minute to her bodice. "Let the Whigs drink what they will — *we'll* toast our King in Champagne."

Anna's hand hovered over the white petals that nestled against her skin and above the wide-brimmed glass her eyes met those of her companion. As she sipped they could have been alone, his nearness shutting out all other sounds and people.

"To you, Anna," he said softly, "my white rose."

Their glasses touched and Anna felt as if all the bubbles had burst inside her head and as her heart pounded against her bodice she wished desperately that she had not allowed herself to be so tightly laced into her corsets. Looking down at her hand, she was surprised to find that she was trembling and hastily replaced the glass on the table, before she should spill any of the sparkling liquid.

"You look like a startled fawn," whispered the man beside her, and avoiding his gaze, she dropped her eyes to her hands, busily pleating the white tablecloth hanging to her knees.

"It's unkind to tease," she said quietly.

Covering one of her hands with his James turned his shoulder to the rest of the company. "I was not teasing," he said soberly and her eyes flew to search his face.

They had removed their masks to eat, but the soft candle glow spread dark shadows and turning away from the lighted table, his face was dark and try how she would, she could not read his expression.

Moistening her lips with the tip of her tongue she took a shaking breath. "I see you wish to flirt," she said lightly, trying to laugh.

"You wrong me, Anna — I was never more serious."

Before she could speak, the company around them rose to their feet declaring their wish to take a turn about the gardens, and James' arm under her elbow contrained her to do the same.

"Nothing could be more pleasant," he said into her ear. "It will be easy to slip away and have a little time to ourselves." Tying the strings of her 'loo' mask behind her head, he pulled up the hood of her rose pink domino and settled it around her neck with a proprietary gesture. "Trust me, Anna," he said softly, smiling down into her eyes.

Outside the booth, the gardens seemed to have filled with people, crowds milling along the paths and making progress increasingly difficult. The men of the party closed around the women, but even so Anna found herself jostled and crushed. Grateful for James' arm, she clung closer, holding down her swaying skirts with one hand, until a sudden surge of the crowd pushed against her, snatching her from the Jacobite's grasp and for a frightening moment she found herself alone among a sea of unfamiliar faces. Suddenly a hand took her arm and, turning in alarm to her supposed attacker, she was confronted by a familiar blue silk cloak.

"James!" she cried in relief. "Thank Heavens you've found me."

One arm encircling her waist, her rescuer hurried her along the path, until the crowds were left behind and Anna found herself in a quiet, darker part of the garden, where the people were few and the flickering overhead lights seemed suddenly ineffectual.

"James, you are going too fast," she panted, almost dragged along by his arm.

As though for answer, he swung away from the main path, plunged through a thickly shrubbed glade and paused on the steps of a small Grecian temple.

Delighted, Anna stared up at the slender pillars and elegant portico of white marble, shining in the moonlight.

"Oh, how pretty," she breathed, turning a glowing countenance to her companion. "It was naughty of you to bring me here, James, but I own that I am glad to have seen it." Touching the clematis that climbed over the building in elegant profusion, she smiled and added impulsively, "though I doubt that we'll find a white rose among these flowers."

The tall figure beside her stiffened perceptibly and glanced down at her, his gaze following her hands as she gently touched the roses at her breast, his pale eyes glinting through the narrow slits of his mask.

Surprised by the way the moonlight drained the colour from his blue eyes,

Anna stared back, suddenly grown uneasy; surely his shoulder was higher than when they had left the dining booth and why should James' mouth be set in such a hard, uncompromising line.

"J-James?" she said, uncertainly, drawing away, her eyes searching his face.

Certain now that the man was not James, she turned to run, but her arm was seized anew and she was hustled up the shallow steps between the pillars and into the temple, before she could do more than draw breath.

"I am sorry to disappoint you," said Captain Bellamy urbanely, before she could release her breath in a scream, "but I am not the amorous James whom you so clearly expected."

Releasing her, he untied the strings of his mask and stood efficiently blocking the entrance, playing with the scrap of black velvet, while he stared at her steadily.

"Wh-what do you want?" demanded Anna, lifting her chin and trying to hide the panic rising in her. "How dare you abduct me like this. Mr Drelincourt will be searching for me — "

"No doubt — but I am afraid that that gentleman must cool his ardour — at least for a moment or two. I believe you have something to say to me, Miss Stanton."

"Nothing — except that I find your manners wanting," retorted Anna, taking refuge in anger.

Captain Bellamy sighed and folding his arms, leaned against an elegant Doric pillar. "Then I am afraid that poor Mr Drelincourt will spend a great deal of time in fruitless search."

Politely hiding her mouth behind her hand, Anna yawned delicately. "*Must* you talk in riddles?" she wondered and retreating to the back of the garden-house, sat on the seat she found there, pointedly turning her shoulder on the man at the entrance.

"You disappoint me. I had supposed that you possessed a modicum of intelligence, but now I find that your brain is turned by a few light words from an amorous adventurer."

Anna turned on him. "James is not like that!" she was betrayed into exclaiming.

The soldier smiled thinly. "He is as

likely to use you for his purposes as any other ambitious man," he told her dryly. "Doubtless he suspects you and chooses this method to waylay your suspicions and gain your loyalty." For a moment he looked down at her averted head, his expression inscrutable, as his eyes travelled over her carefully schooled features, only the movement of the roses on her bodice betraying her emotions.

"Come, Anna," he said impatiently. "Ben told me weeks ago of the arrival of the mysterious stranger on the night of Lady Primrose's soirée."

Staring at him, wide eyed, the girl arched her eyebrows.

"Mysterious?" she repeated. "On a night when so many guests called at Essex Street, how can one be termed 'mysterious'? I believe Ben has too much imagination."

The heavy folds of his cloak whispered as he crossed the floor swiftly and stood over her, a dark shadow silhouetted by the light from the garden.

"I want to know what was said among the gentlemen who stayed behind after the evening party," he said, a hint of menace in his quiet voice.

"I am afraid I went to bed — "

Hard hands gripped her arms above the elbows and dragged her to her feet. "Don't be brave with your brother's life," warned the soldier, harshly. "Or have you thrown off your sisterly love and grown a new loyalty?" Feeling the girl shiver under his hands, he pressed home his advantage. "Remember your brother can easily be recalled from his regiment if I lodge a summons against him. He won't thank you if he finds himself in debtors' gaol."

"I h-hate you," cried Anna beating impotent hands against her captor's chest, and railing against her size and sex. "How I wish I was a man — "

A grim smile crossed the face above her and possessing himself of both her hands, held her until she grew calmer.

At last something like a sob escaped her and she hung her head, hiding her face in the shadow of her deep hood.

After a while he released her and turned away, looking out over the quiet garden. When he spoke, his voice made the girl start and lift her head sharply.

"I know about the purchase of muskets and weapons in Antwerp," he said surprisingly, his voice clear and cool, "but I need to know just who is involved. I'll wager that a list was made to send to the Prince — " Turning suddenly, he read the answer in her face before she could control her expression. "I thought so," he breathed satisfied with his ruse. "Then, Miss Stanton, I must ask you to procure me a copy of that interesting document."

"I — can't," exclaimed Anna, dismay in her voice.

"You must," she was told implacably, and reading the hard eyes directed at her, Anna knew the threat behind the words and lowered her own gaze in silent acquiescence.

"You — ask too much," she whispered, huddled despairingly in her gay pink domino. "I shall be found out."

"I hope not," Rafe Bellamy murmured, "for your sake — I've a feeling James Drelincourt would not be kind to any who got in his way or proved an encumbrance."

Anna thought of the ruthless twist

to his mouth that she had seen upon occasions and felt a chill slip down her spine, even as she tried to convince herself that James obviously cared for her and was almost on the point of declaring himself. Reminding herself of his words and actions earlier that evening she tried to draw comfort from the thought and said bravely,

"No-one could be so cruel and hard as you."

"No?" He considered the matter. "But then I have the trump card, my dear — remember I hold your brother's bills."

"You are hardly likely to let me forget," she answered bitterly.

"No," he agreed and looked down at her thoughtfully. "Take my advice, Anna," he said in a changed tone, "and don't allow yourself to become entangled with our Jacobite friend. Remember that neither he nor I are what the polite world would call honourable men. We use people for our advantage — and take care that we are not the ones to be hurt."

Pointing her chin, Anna stared at him coldly. "I have no need of your advice, Captain Bellamy — I refuse to believe that James is anything but honourable — "

"You may be forced to believe."

Jumping to her feet, her anger suddenly overcoming her fear and caution, Anna faced him. "Never! He loves me!"

Grey eyes widened slightly, his attention caught by her announcement, before his mouth curved into a cool smile. "My poor innocent," he said pityingly. "I am afraid you have a great deal to learn."

Blinking back angry tears, Anna stamped her foot. "You are intolerable," she told the man before her fiercely. "You believe in no-one. You have no trust — no human feelings. You're made of iron like one of those automatons the Germans are always making — someone winds you up and you do what you're told without regard or thought of the consequence."

If she had looked up, she would have seen that Rafe Bellamy was regarding her with a curious expression, but she was so intent upon fighting back her tears and trying to find words with which to devastate her opponent, that she could

176

do no more than glance at him briefly as she dashed the tears away with the back of her hand.

"I — w-will not work for you," she said, more quietly, her voice trembling. "I will not spy — and betray my friends any more. I have done enough — I despise myself." Suddenly she looked up, her face white in the light from the moon, teardrops spiking her dark lashes. "You make me feel — unclean!"

With a stifled sob, she knocked away the hand he stretched out to her, dodged round his detaining arm and before he could stop her, had dashed from the temple.

The lateness of the hour had thinned the crowds but Anna hid in the depths of her cloak as she ran along, hoping to hide from the curious stares her hurry aroused. She seemed to have been seeking her party for hours and the search had begun to take on the substance of a nightmare, when a voice called her name and hands clutched at the silk of her domino.

With a cry of fright, she tried to break away, before she recognised James' anxious face and regardless of convention, flung herself into his arms.

"Oh, take me away," she sobbed against his chest. "Please take me home!"

7

LUCKILY her agitation was put down to her having become separated from the rest of the party and accepted as right and proper for a delicately nurtured female under the circumstances.

Anna spent a worried and restless night, but arose from her bed the next morning with her resolution still intact; she would *not* spy on the Drelincourt household for Captain Bellamy again and with this in mind she arranged a call on Mrs Masham the milliner in the Strand.

It proved easy to wait until Cessy was busy with her own affairs and then to remember a hat that was needed quickly for an outing.

"Of course," agreed the Irish girl, "but pray take Betty. Aunt Anne nearly had the vapours when she discovered that you had been out alone before."

The little maid proved a cheerful

companion, tripping along beside Anna and regaling her with gossip about their masters and mistresses gleaned from other servants.

Waiting until the shop was empty except for themselves, Anna recalled a set of ribbons she needed and sent Betty across the street to the large emporium opposite, then turned to Mrs Masham, who was eyeing her in a speculative manner.

"I won't beat about the bush Mrs Masham," she said positively. "From talk I have heard among your customers, I believe you might be able to help me — I have need of a money-lender."

Mrs Masham's eyebrows rose and she half smiled. "I admire your bluntness, miss," she said. "Time wasted is time lost, I always say. D'you need a lot or just a bit of the ready?"

"A — lot," Anna told her calmly.

The other woman whistled through her pursed lips. "Well, you're a calm one, I must say."

She turned away and began rolling tangled lengths of ribbon round her fingers. Anna watched her busy, plump hands, conscious of the need for haste before Betty returned and at last could bear no more.

"Can you help me?" she burst out, her voice inordinately loud in the small shop.

The milliner looked up, her fingers stilled among the laces and ribbons she was tidying.

"I may see my way to assisting you, miss," she said, "but it'll take time and trouble on my part." She smiled slightly, her eyes cool and watchful, "and time is money, my dear."

"I'll — pay you," said Anna and at once the plump hand was held out and she dropped the guinea she had ready into the woman's palm.

Mrs Masham looked at the gold coin glinting against her skin and shook her head. "Not enough, my dear," she said and waited expectantly.

Reluctantly Anna dropped another coin into her waiting hand and as she did so the door behind them opened as Betty returned from her errand.

At once the money vanished into the depths of the milliner's capacious pocket hanging under her skirt and she spoke to Anna in an ordinary voice as though nothing untoward had passed between them.

"I'll let you know tomorrow, miss. I'll send my girl with a message."

Wondering if she had lost her money uselessly, Anna left the shop, grateful for the maid's presence, but not listening to her bright chatter.

How wise she had been in seeking assistance was proved the next day, when not only the expected note from the milliner appeared on her breakfast tray, but also a missive from Kit. With a sinking heart she tore it open and read the spiky writing, blotted and blurred with the writer's agitation.

The few lines told her that he had been put under arrest for debt — far from blaming Captain Bellamy for his predicament, Kit urged her sympathy for the soldier, saying that he must be in dire straits to have sold the billet bonx to whoever had foreclosed on them.

'However difficult for you, dear Ann,' he had written, 'I must ask you to help me in this matter. I have two days to settle the matter, before the Army discharges me to debtors' prison.'

The paper slipped from her nerveless fingers and fluttered to the floor, while the girl stared blankly into space, her face pale and despairing. Suddenly recalling the other letter, she searched feverishly among the disordered bedclothes to find it.

'Monsieur Diablo will see you an hour before noon today — you will find him at the sign of the Ship of Fortune in Cheapside.'

Thrusting both papers out of sight in one of her drawers, Anna began to dress, her hands trembling so much that she could hardly tie the strings or fasten the hooks of her gown.

By great good fortune the inmates of the house in Essex Street seemed intent upon their own affairs that day and shortly after mid-morning Anna was able to slip out of the house, muffled in her cloak and hurry to the end of the road, almost certain that no-one had seen her.

"'Lo, miss," said a voice cheerfully and looking down she found Ben Bow by her side.

"G–go away," she whispered, making little shooing gestures, but suddenly realising he might be useful, reached out and seized a skinny arm. "Can you find me a coach?" she asked.

His eyes widened. "Coo — you eloping?"

"No — of course not," she answered impatiently, glancing over her shoulder to the corner that hid Essex Street. "Will you fetch me a carriage, or not?"

He hopped from one bare, dirty foot to the other. "You'll have to tell me where you want to go — the Jarveys all has their own parts of London, like."

"Cheapside — the Ship of Fortune."

Suddenly he grew still, his head on one side as he regarded her. "That's old Diablo's place," he said slowly. "You don't want to tangle with him, miss."

"I'll give you a penny if you go for a coach."

Hesitating, indecision in his expression, he bit his thumb.

"Oh, very well," snapped Anna, setting off again, "I'll manage for myself."

"No, miss. I'll do it, honest I will," cried the boy, running at her heels and clutching her cloak. "You wait here and I'll be back as quick as I can."

Anna watched his retreating back, shrinking against the nearby wall to make herself as inconspicuous as possible. She had scarcely time to grow impatient before a decrepit vehicle came into view and Ben jumped down as it stopped beside her.

Dropping the promised coin into his outstretched hand, the girl climbed into the coach, giving instructions to the driver before she closed the door. Her last glimpse of Ben was of him running wildly in the opposite direction and she smiled a little at the thought of his eagerness to spend her penny.

The driver refused to wait, demanding his fare and driving off almost as soon as her foot touched the ground, leaving Anna examining the building before her with growing apprehension.

The street in which she found herself was old and sombre, with none of the charm that comes with age, rather the ancient buildings exuded an air of threatening menace, seeming to crowd upon her, each house and crooked roof appearing to peer down at the stranger. Shivering, Anna drew her cloak closer about her shoulders, certain that countless eyes were staring at her from the many dark and dingy windows.

The weathered sign above her head creaked and lifting her eyes she could barely make out the picture of a ship coming into port. With a tentative hand she pushed the door and found herself at the foot of a long, steep flight of stairs. Lifting her skirts out of the accumulation of dust and dirt, she began to climb, her mouth uncomfortably dry and her heart beating a rapid tattoo against her ribs. The boards under her feet creaked and groaned with each step, giving notice to all of her progress and she was unhappily aware that whoever awaited her was well notified of her arrival.

The door at the head of the stairs was as dark and grime-encrusted as the rest of the house, but the room in which she found herself brought her up in surprise; panelled walls gleamed dully in the light from the wide, mullioned window, while the furniture could have come from Lady Primrose's house in Essex Street. To

186

her utter amazement everything about the room spoke of wealth and taste. A heavy oak table faced the door and, a movement drawing her attention to it, she saw that which she had missed in her quick scrutiny of the surprising room.

A man dressed entirely in black sat behind the table, a large ledger open in front of him and a sheaf of papers close to hand. Used as she was to the bright colours of the fashionable world, his clothing appeared unusual to Anna and, raising her eyes to his face, she was at once struck by something even more odd — in an age when all men wore powder and most men wore wigs, he not only obviously wore his own hair, but that hair was so dark as to appear black and was totally without the slightest sprinkling of white. The effect was unusual to say the least and even as she examined him, the man lifted his head and looked fully at her, his pale skin contrasting unpleasantly with the sombreness of his dress and hair.

"Come in, Miss Stanton," he said, laying aside his quill. "I understand you would have business with me."

"Y-yes." Anna took the seat he indicated, trying to appear calm and collected, "I wish to borrow some money. Two thousand guineas, in fact."

He nodded understandingly and put the tips of his fingers together in an arch. "Just so — and of course you have some security to offer?"

Anna had thought of this and silently produced her mother's pearls and held them out. Taking them from her, Monsieur Diablo went to the window and examined them. Returning he dropped them contemptuously on the polished surface of the table.

"I think you are playing with me," he remarked pleasantly, something in his tone making the hair on the back of Anna's neck tingle.

"Wh-what do you mean?" she stammered.

"These," he touched the pearls with a finger, "are worth nothing." His eyes flickered over her, taking in the brocade gown under her cloak and the lace that peeped from under her skirt. "My clients are not poor, Miss Stanton. For Mrs Masham to have sent you here, you must have rich relations or the promise of wealth to come."

Miserably, Anna swallowed. "I — have no-one."

The man in black picked up his pen. "Then we cannot do business," he said, dismissing her.

Anna looked at the dark bent head and decided to try again. "I — have friends," she said.

The man appeared uninterested, his quill scratching steadily across the page. "Don't waste my time," he advised, not looking up.

"I know several titled people," said Anna desperately. "Indeed at this moment, I am staying in Essex Street . . . with a lady of rank and wealth."

Dropping the pen again, the man opposite leaned back in his chair and smiled in a manner which reminded Anna forcibly of an illustration she had once seen of a scene from Red Riding Hood.

"My dear Miss Stanton," he said, "you cannot really expect me to advance you the sum of two thousand guineas without knowing the name of your lady of rank."

Glancing away, Anna bit her lip,

unwilling to give him her benefactress's name and yet seeing no other way of obtaining the money she needed. "Lady Primrose," she said reluctantly, at last and knew she had caught the other's interest for he was staring at her with undisguised speculation.

"In-deed," he breathed, thoughtfully. "And this lady, you say, is very fond of you?"

"V-very," said Anna, hoping to impress him.

"And Lady Primrose, all London knows, is extremely rich."

"Extremely," agreed Anna and saw at once her mistake, for now Monsieur Diablo was looking at her with what only could be described as a proprietary air. "Well, not as wealthy as all that," she added hastily. "I daresay she's not rich at all, really."

Showing his teeth in a thin smile, the money-lender stood up. "In a minute you'll be telling me that she has no tenderness for you."

"How did you guess? I'm sorry to have tried to deceive you — I can see that you were too clever to have been taken in.

I'm only companion to Lady Primrose's niece." His smile took on a decidedly unpleasant air. "You'd be wise not to play with me."

"No — yes. I won't again. I'm truly sorry to have bothered you." Anna was on her feet and taking a surreptitious step towards the door behind her.

Without seeming to move Monsieur Diablo was beside her, much too close and looking at his face, Anna could suddenly see how he had earned his name.

"I've a friend waiting," she said, backing away.

He shook his head. "The coachman drove off — do you think I don't have my spies to tell me all I want to know? You were foolish enough to venture here quite alone, Miss Stanton."

Suddenly Anna spun on her heels, her skirts flaring out and ran for the door. Even as her hands scrabbled on the latch, she was seized from behind and dragged back. With surprising strength, Monsieur Diablo held her against him, quelling her struggle easily.

"Scream, Miss Stanton," he said into

191

her ear, something in his voice telling Anna that he was enjoying himself, "No-one will come to your aid. The inhabitants of this area are quite used to female screams."

Anna closed her eyes and grew very still, suddenly more afraid that she had ever been, knowing that Rafe Bellamy had never engendered such fear as she now felt and even while a shudder of sheer terror ran down her spine, they both heard the warning creak as someone climbed the stairs.

Thin fingers closed cruelly over her mouth. "Visitors — could it be a friend of yours?" hissed Monsieur Diablo. "Don't be stupid enough to make a sound." He brought his free hand up, allowing Anna to see the small, businesslike pistol that he held.

The room was silent as they waited, the muffled sounds growing nearer until, suddenly, three quick taps seemed startlingly loud as someone rapped against the door in a definite rhythm.

Anna felt the man holding her relax slightly. "My friend — not yours," he breathed.

The latch lifted and the door swung gently open. "While I know we cannot be termed bosom friends, Diablo, I hardly fancy my entrance demands such a welcome," said Captain Bellamy, eyeing the pistol with disfavour.

Coming into the room, he kicked the door to behind him and, ignoring Anna, gave his attention to the man in black.

"Bellamy!" exclaimed the money-lender. "What do you here?"

"I've come for the girl," the other answered easily.

Diablo's arm, tightened. He had released his grip on the girl's mouth at the soldier's entrance, but his arm had fallen to her waist and now he held her in front of him in a painful grasp.

"She's mine," he said. "If she's not worth a ransom — there are other ways in which she can earn me a penny or two."

"She works for me," Rafe Bellamy told him, leaning his broad shoulders against the panels of the door behind him. His position was negligent but his eyes were intent and watchful.

"*Works* for you!" the man was openly

incredulous. "D'you expect me to believe she plays the same game as you? A soft, silk and satin miss." He laughed harshly. "More like she's your doxy."

Broad shoulders under orange velvet shrugged. "Believe what you will," he said indifferently. "Mistress or not she leaves here with me."

Standing very still in the circle of the black arm, Anna felt that both men had forgotten her presence, so intent were they upon each other as antagonism flared between them.

"For you to have come yourself, Captain Bellamy, like some knight errant of old, only confirms my original surmise — the girl is valuable."

"More valuable than our business dealings together? Would you lose them for a surmise? I had thought you more astute, Diablo."

The money-lender stared across the room, trying to read the other's expression. For a moment he appeared undecided, then shook his head slightly. "My friend, if you had sent a minion sometime later, I would have believed you, but to have come yourself and so swiftly, only confirms my original impression, but being a reasonable man, I am prepared to deal with you. In view of our old acquaintance, I'll allow you twenty-five per cent of what she fetches."

Captain Bellamy straightened. "She's worthless," he said grimly, "but nevertheless I intend to take her with me, when I go."

"My dear Bellamy, I believe you are in love," sneered the other softly, bringing up the pistol he had held all this while, as the soldier began to move.

Anna had been watching intently, deceiving by her quietness the man who held her into believing that she was frightened into submissiveness. For all Captain Bellamy's negligent attitude, she had seen the tenseness behind his manner and at first sign of movement, she brought the sharp heel of her shoe down upon the instep of the man behind her.

With a cry of pain, Monsieur Diablo flung her from him, sending her hurtling into a corner as Rafe Bellamy seized his arm and wrenched the pistol from his grasp. With the same motion the soldier's arm continued on its way, and the pistol connected sharply with the money-lender's pale pointed chin.

Without a sound Monsieur Diablo slithered to the floor, lying still and limp at his assailant's feet.

Anna's hands were taken and she was set on her feet in a flurry of petticoats with scant regard for dignity.

"You did that to the manner born, but now we must be on our way," Captain Bellamy told her, thrusting the loose papers from the table into his deep pockets. Carrying the heavy ledger, he caught her arm and hurried her to the door, pausing for a quick look about the room and at the supine figure in the middle of the floor. "Our friend's acquaintances will be on their way," he said grimly and something in his tone made the girl pick up her skirts and obey him wordlessly.

A decrepit coach, the twin of the vehicle which had brought her to the Ship of Fortune, but which Anna had no difficulty in recognising as Captain Bellamy's favourite mode of transport, was waiting. A hand under her elbow thrust her into the capacious depths, the horses were whipped up and the coach was in motion before the passengers had seated themselves.

Huddled in her corner, Anna closed her eyes and felt sick, unable to control her trembling limbs now that the danger was passed.

"What in God's name induced you to go to that Hell hole?" demanded her companion suddenly.

Anna opened her eyes, but sight of his angry countenance made her close them again, and try as she would, she could not prevent two fat tears from slipping out from under her lashes and sliding down her cheeks.

Captain Bellamy sighed impatiently. "Oh, I know full well *why* you went, but surely you could have chosen someone other than the most notorious Devil in all of London?"

Opening her eyes Anna stared at him indignantly. "Mrs Masham sent me — she's your friend. How was I to know — "

"Mrs Masham is hardly a friend. — I make use of her at times."

"Like that — that fiend, I suppose."

"Diablo had his uses, but I've long wanted to see inside his book — I've a notion that the names of some of his clients will surprise even me. All is not lost, Miss Stanton, I do assure you."

"I'm g-glad to hear it," said Anna bitterly and suddenly to her utter dismay, found herself quite unable to restrain the sobs that shook her. Hiding her face, she turned into her corner of the coach and cried unrestrainedly. At last, when she showed signs of regaining control, a large lace-edged handkerchief was dropped into her lap. Using it gratefully Anna glanced at her companion behind its enveloping folds and found his surveying her with an expression she could not read.

"Better, Miss Stanton?" he asked, not unkindly.

"You f-foreclosed on Kit," accused Anna, returning to the most important item on her mind.

"Indeed I did — but I hoped only to spur you into doing what I wanted, not to goad you into such a dangerous course of action."

"Did you think I'd take meekly to such a thing?" she asked fiercely.

"I should have known better," he told her a smile at the back of his eyes as he watched her.

Her brief moment of anger over, Anna subsided miserably into her corner, shaken now and again by a half stifled sob.

Captain Bellamy regarded her for a few moments, before reaching forward, he took both her hands in his. Surprised by his action, Anna looked up, after the initial resistance allowing her hands to lie passively in his grasp.

"Miss Stanton — Anna, cannot we come to some agreement?" She did not answer, merely shook her head slightly as he went on. "If I cannot bully and blackmail you into spying on the Drelincourts, I shall do something, which perhaps I'd have been wiser to do from the first and that is to persuade you of the right of what I ask."

His grip was warm as he held her hands, and in the confines of the coach Anna found herself unable to look away from his intense, grey gaze. Eyes wide, she listened with parted lips and quickened breath to his insistent voice.

"Do you remember the tales you've heard about the Great Rebellion? How families were divided by conflicting loyalties and how father and brother fought bitter battles convinced that either Cromwell or the King were right? It took us nearly a hundred years to recover from that war and the Jacobites would plunge us into another civil conflict. They did their best five years ago in Scotland, but by the Grace of God, their machinations came to naught and now James Drelincourt and his cronies are doing their utmost to prepare the ground for another Stuart landing — but here in London which, if it succeeds, will bring death and turmoil in its wake."

His grip on her hands tightened until she winced slightly as he pulled her forward a little on the seat until their faces were only inches apart.

"And that Anna Stanton, is something I intend to prevent."

Anna licked dry lips. "Would it really be so bad?" she whispered.

"Worse than anything you can imagine," he told her. "We have a Hanoverian on the throne and a settled, stable Kingdom.

If I can prevent it, nothing will be allowed to mar the contented lives of my countrymen. Whatever I may feel personally about the rights of the Stuarts, I will accept George of Hanover rather than see Civil War split England again."

Anna stared up at him, studying his face silently as the coach lurched over the cobblestones. Never having considered the consequences of a Stuart uprising, she was dismayed to find herself agreeing with him. "But Charles Edward Stuart is — " she felt obliged to protest.

"The stuff of dreams," supplied Rafe Bellamy, smiling. "He is romance and adventure, the cause for which every young man would shed his blood. But sensible people settle for less — or more. I want a home to come back to, not a blackened shell, burnt because opposing soldiers passed that way."

"I cannot spy on James — on the Drelincourts. I am too involved. They are my friends — can't you understand?" Her voice died away under his steady gaze and she dropped her eyes to her hands straining together in her lap. "Send me somewhere else," she pleaded. "I'll work for you anywhere, but here."

"My dear you are too useful. You have the entrée," said her companion, aware of her conflicting emotions, "but once this affair is concluded you have my word that I shall ask no more of you."

She looked at him with renewed hope. "Your word. I have your word?" she said eager to seize any chance however small of finding a way out of her difficulties.

"Remember Kit," warned Captain Bellamy, reading her fleeting expressions. "In return for my promise, I shall require your word to work for me loyally until I release you from your obligation."

"You have it," said Anna, hiding her reluctance.

Her companion sighed and relaxed against his seat. "Now, there is the little matter of a certain paper which interests me," he said.

Anna looked at him steadily. "Also the small matter of my brother's bills?" she reminded him bravely.

"It shall be seen to — as soon as you send me a copy of the list of Jacobites."

Anna's heart sank. "H-he only had

until tomorrow — "

"All the more reason for speed on your part," her companion pointed out. "Ben will be waiting for a message — don't disappoint him."

Silence fell in the coach as it lumbered on its way, until it drew to a halt in a road that seemed familiar to Anna.

"We are a few yards from Essex Street," the soldier told her, opening the door and lowering the steps. Stepping out onto the road, he offered her his hand retaining hers after she had descended from the rickety vehicle.

"My apologies — I am truly sorry that you had such an unhappy experience this morning."

Anna looked up shivering slightly at the memory of the money-lender for the first time aware of Rafe Bellamy's sympathy. "I had no idea that such people existed — not money-lenders, of course, I know about them — but such people. He was like a spider, waiting in his web. And his name — at first it made me laugh, but once I'd met him, it was too applicable to be amusing." She paused and glanced up again, her lips curving in a tired smile. "I believe you might have done me a good turn — however much I need money in future, you may be sure I will never turn to a money-lender for it!" she said, candidly.

Sketching a bow, he stepped back as she walked away, not climbing into the waiting coach until she had turned the corner into Essex Street.

Anna found her absence had not been remarked upon, James being out about his own affairs and Cecilia and Lady Primrose intent upon the business of arranging an outing to the little village of Kensington. They looked up at her entrance, eager to tell her of their arrangements.

"An all day affair, I think," said Lady Primrose. "We shall take the carriage as I like to be comfortable, but you girls may ride, if you wish."

"Faith, I find such an idea delightful!" exclaimed the Irish girl, turning shining eyes towards Anna. "What of you, my love, do you ride?"

"In the country one has to, but I've not been on horseback since coming to London," confessed Anna, scarcely able to believe that she could be taking part in such an ordinary conversation after the events of the morning.

"You can borrow one of my habits," offered Cessy promptly with her customary generosity. "I've one put away which I've never liked," she added, laughing at herself.

"We shall ask several of our acquaintances," put in Lady Primrose, "and make it quite a large affair. I daresay there will be quite a few whom you'll not have met."

Anna caught the glance Cecilia and her aunt exchanged. If her senses had not been heightened by her experiences, she would have thought nothing of it, but having lived her strange, unnatural life for several months, she was attuned to nuances in the air and now observed her companions carefully.

"I always think it a good thing for young folk to know as many people as possible," went on the older woman. "Of course not all will be our actual friends, Anna, and I wouldn't like you to think they were. People in our position have a great many *acquaintances*, people one has met and perhaps owes some slight hospitality."

"I see," Anna said doubtfully into the pause, feeling that something was required of her.

"Pray don't go on so, Aunt," interposed her niece. "I am sure Anna is well aware of what you mean."

Smiling, Anna nodded agreement, but privately wondered at Lady Primrose's meaning. Surely she had been a little *too* insistent about her guests not being friends and later, Anna found herself examining the list of expected guests with more than usual interest, but after a quick perusal of the crabbed writing she had to admit that as far as she could tell no-one of great importance had been invited. The only Jacobites of wealth and importance she knew of, the Duke of Beaufort and the Earl of Westmorland, powerful nobles who made no attempt to hide their allegiance, were conspicuous by their absence, and she folded the paper, forced to conclude that she had been mistaken in her surmisings.

August weather was particularly hot and Lady Primrose and her niece retiring to their respective bedchambers that afternoon and James still being out of the house, Anna was presented with the perfect opportunity to search for his incriminating list. After a moment's thought, she picked up her skirts and sped along the passage to the room beside the garden door as being the most likely hiding place.

Closing the door silently, she leaned against its panels, feeling their coolness against her back, as she surveyed the room. Hopefully discarding the books lining the shelves, her eye alighted on an inlaid walnut escritoire and she hurried across the floor to pull out the many small drawers and search feverishly among their contents.

It did not take her many moments to realise that the list was not there, and she turned her full attention upon the one locked drawer, certain that James would not have left so incriminating an article loose for all to examine. Try as she would, she could not open the drawer and half crying with frustration and annoyance, she seized the desk flap and gave the whole piece of furniture a furious shake.

To her amazement the key, which must have been secreted somewhere among the ornate decorations and curlicues, fell at her feet. With a smothered exclamation of relief, she snatched it up, thrust it into the lock and pulled out the drawer, her fingers scrabbling among the papers in its interior.

Seizing a sheet of paper from the desk she hastily copied down the list of names, her heart beating fast all the while at the thought of discovery. Footsteps in the passage made her pause, her breath quickening until they passed, but at last she had finished and pushing all the papers back into the drawer, she locked it and returned the escritoire to as near the appearance it had presented before she had attacked it.

The key gave her pause and she held it in her palm wondering what to do with it, while her eye searched the carvings for the possible hiding place. At last she dropped it onto the floor, hoping that the next person to look for it would suppose it had fallen there.

Hiding the folded paper among the folds of her wide skirts, she cautiously left the room. The hall was empty and it was the work of moments to open the front door and for Ben to run across the road at her urgent signal. Deliberately closing her mind to what she was doing, Anna thrust the paper into his hands, whispered hasty instructions and shut the door again, leaning her forehead for a second on its dark woodwork before, straightening her shoulders with an obvious effort, she turned and slowly mounted the stairs.

8

"I CAN'T take it," said Anna decisively, when a few days later Cecilia brought a velvet riding-habit to her room and offered it to her as a gift.

"Whyever not?" asked the other girl in surprise.

"Y-you've given me enough — too much. I really can't accept any more."

"Sure and I don't see why not, when it gives me pleasure to give it to you. Aren't we friends?"

"Yes — of course, but — "

"Then, it's your stiff-necked English pride that's the cause, is it?" the Irish girl demanded, her eyes beginning to sparkle, as she flung the habit on the bed.

"No, it's not that," answered Anna unhappily.

"Then for the Lord's sake, what is it?"

Anna swallowed and looked away. "You're all too kind . . . I don't deserve

210

it," she said in a small voice, examining her fingernails intently.

"Faith, is that all!" exclaimed Cecilia, plonking herself down on the bed, beside the crumpled velvet skirt. "Don't you know the pleasure you've given us all? You've taken a load off Aunt Anne's shoulders. I'm afraid she never cared for the role of Duenna to me, you've been the sister I've never had and as for James — well, I'd best leave him to speak for himself, but I'm sure you must know that he thinks very highly of you."

Slowly turning her head, Anna met her eyes and for a moment the two girls exchanged glances, before the fair girl, patted the velvet folds and smiled up at the other.

"You'll take it won't you?" she wheedled. "To please me."

"We-ll," Anna was lost for words and made an uncomfortable little gesture which the other at once took for assent.

"Good — even I can see that violet isn't my colour, though it will become you charmingly. I shall wear my green habit — it's new and has a delightful tricorn hat to go with it, with an ostrich plume in the brim. I can tell you, my love, that we shall put all the other beauties to shame."

Anna was still uncomfortable about accepting the gift when the day of the outing arrived, but as she hooked the tight jacket and glanced in the mirror she had to admit that the colour and masculine style suited her; with her hair tied back by a black ribbon, a hat trimmed with silver lace set firmly on her head and her chin nestling among the snowy folds of a cravat, the face that looked back at her might have been that of a handsome boy. Giving an ironical salute to her reflection, she picked up the long, heavy folds of her skirt and hurried down to the hall.

Admiration gleamed plainly in James' eyes as he came to give her his hand down the last few steps.

"How glad I am that my Aunt arranged this outing," he said, carrying her hand to his lips.

"I would have thought that such an event was held to be quite ordinary to a gentleman — especially one who rides the countryside as much as you," she answered demurely.

He laughed and nipped her fingers. "'Tis the company that makes the difference," he assured her. "I've arranged for Jason Weston to keep my sister out of mischief, and with Lady Primrose comfortably ensconced in her carriage, you and I, Anna, should be allowed some time to ourselves."

A thrill of pleasure scurried down her spine, but the look she sent him was a little troubled. She would have liked his intentions to be clearer, but until he declared himself, she was bound by convention and could not ask what his feelings were regarding herself. His actions were such as to make her suppose herself the object of his affections, but her good sense told her that he could not want a wife with neither dowry or position and while he showed her every attention, he had been very reticent when it came to the actual point of declaring his feelings.

If only she could be certain of his love, many of the troubles that beset her would be miraculously cleared, she thought, pulling on her gloves. She could tell him about Rafe Bellamy and his machinations and be free of the burden of guilt that weighed so heavily upon her conscience.

James seemed unaware of her preoccupation and turned away to marshal his small force. Lady Primrose and another lady were seated in the heavy coach, while the grooms brought up the riders' mounts and Anna found herself seated on a small grey mare, while Cecilia rode a showy chestnut.

For a few minutes the street seemed crowded with horses and riders, then the party sorted itself into some kind of order and, at a laughing order from James, started off towards the Bath Road.

Cecilia's chestnut, as well as being handsome, was obviously high-spirited, showing his nervousness by pulling at the bit and dancing a little whenever they passed anything to which he decided to take exception. While admiring the ease with which the Irish girl handled him, Anna was thankful for the calm of her own mount and reaching forward patted the warm, grey neck with sudden gratitude.

The late August sun shone warmly on the magnificent façade of Buckingham House as they rode past and Anna could not resist gazing in awe at the enormous building as she wondered at the wealth and style of the people who could afford to live in such splendour.

Approaching Knightsbridge, which until lately had been a separate village, the spirits of the party rose at the prospect of the holiday that awaited them and soon chatter and laughter filled the air as they rode out of the city and into the awaiting countryside.

The little village of Kensington was reached about noon, the party clattering down the main street to stop at the inn, where the landlord waited on his doorstep to greet them, bowing and smiling as he offered the hospitality of his house.

A cold collation was set out in the parlour, while a table waited in the garden for those who preferred the novelty of eating in the open air and leaving the two older ladies and the staider members of the party in the seclusion of the inn, the younger people soon filed out into the sunshine. When the meal was over the party broke up into groups, some remaining in the garden to enjoy the sun and some more energetically exploring the quiet village and its surroundings.

Strolling with Cecilia, Anna caught sight of James ahead of them deep in conversation with two fashionably dressed ladies. She had noticed them before and, not having been introduced, could contain her curiosity no longer and turning to her companion asked their names.

"Where?" demanded the Irish girl, looking ahead just as James turned a corner and vanished from sight. "I didn't see — just two acquaintances, I suppose."

Anna looked at her friend. She was almost sure that Cecilia had seen her brother ahead and had walked slower to lengthen the gap between them.

"Two handsome girls," she persisted. "One in a blue habit and the other in mustard yellow. You *must* have seen them."

Cecilia shrugged. "What does it matter? Perhaps they are friends of friends. It's very easy to gate-crash a party such as this."

"But — "

"Faith, Anna, I begin to think you're showing signs of jealousy!"

"I am in no position to do any such thing," said Anna stiffly. "I was merely curious, not having met them before or seen them among your acquaintances."

Coming up with a group who proposed to explore a nearby coppice the matter was dropped but the puzzle remained to plague her, until sometime later she found herself alone with Ensign Weston and took the opportunity to casually turn the conversation in the required direction.

He frowned. "Two girls in mustard and blue," he pondered, then his brow cleared. "You must mean Catherine and Clementina Walkinshaw! You're right, we don't usually see them. Catherine is in the service of the Princess of Wales. I suppose her duties keep her busy."

"How interesting," said Anna, thoughtfully. "I've never even seen any of the Royal family."

"It's not surprising. Take my word

for it, the King's court is deadly dull, and the Prince of Wales holds his own minor court at Leicester House for all his own cronies. Neither would provide an evening of merit, I assure you."

Anna laughed. "You're very plain. Do I take it that you're not a Royalist?"

"I'm a soldier, Miss Anna," Jason told her forthrightly. "Politics don't interest me and can be dangerous. I steer clear of them."

"How wise. Let us talk of something else. Do you intend to visit your mother this summer?"

"She and the children intend to spend a few days in London later this month. I would be happy if I could introduce them to you and Miss Cecilia."

"I should like that above all and I'm sure Cessy would be only too happy to meet your family."

He smiled disarmingly down at her. "Do you really think so?"

He would have said more, but James bore down on them and by some adroit method of his own, soon had Anna to himself while the Ensign went in search of Cecilia.

"There," said James, a hint of triumph in his voice as he led the girl into the seclusion of the shade cast by a huge oak tree, "I told you we would have the opportunity of a moment's privacy."

"Your aunt would not think it proper — "

"I am very fond of Aunt Anne, but for once she may go hang!" Taking off his hat, he flung it to the ground at his feet and stepping quickly forward took both Anna's hands in his. "You don't know how I've longed to be alone with you," he said, quietly, dropping a kiss into each palm.

Anna stared up into his handsome, tanned face, feeling herself drowning in his bright blue gaze as he removed the tricorn from her head and dropped it carelessly to join his in the grass. Wordlessly, she reached up and touched his brown cheek, sliding her finger across his chin to lightly caress the strong curves of his mouth.

Suddenly he pulled her into his arms, tilting up her chin impatiently to find her mouth with his. Anna felt herself melting beneath his touch as the trees and surrounding countryside retreated into unimportance. She could feel the heavy, beat of his heart and knew that her own was trying to break free from the confines of the tight corset beneath the velvet jacket she wore.

At last he raised his head and released her a little. Bruised and shaken, the world began to right itself and she smiled, breathlessly.

"J-James — "

His eyes darkened and his grip tightened again, but before he could draw her to him, a wild commotion in the village carried to their ears and startled, they both listened.

Masculine shouts and female screams carried clearly on the still air, while Cessy wildly calling Jason Weston's name could be heard above all.

For a moment their eyes met in bewilderment, before releasing her, James snatched up his hat and clapping it on his head ran in the direction of the noise.

Following him, Anna could not help a gasp of dismay at the sight which met her; a wildly milling crowd surrounded Cecilia who was kneeling beside the still figure of the young soldier as he lay sprawled in the dusty road. Clasping his limp hand, the Irish girl was repeatedly calling his name and begging him to wake up, with an urgency that betrayed her feelings.

As she hurried forward, Anna saw James on one knee beside his friend, examining his head with gentle fingers. Reaching Cecilia she took her by the shoulders and tried to calm her.

"Hush, now," she soothed. "Let James see. I'm sure he knows about such things."

Anxious eyes watched while the slim, brown fingers explored the soldier's cropped head, the discarded wig and hat, making their owner seem young and vulnerable.

"James?" cried Cecilia, frightened by her brother's serious face and abstracted manner.

Looking at her briefly, he made a gesture for her to be silent, while he pulled up the lax eyelids and felt the pulse.

"I don't think there's a fracture," he announced at last, his voice grave, "but he's probably concussed and one arm is broke." Looking across at Anna he smiled for her alone. "Take care of Cessy," he said, before beginning to give orders for the safe removal of his friend.

"Come," said Anna, urging Cecilia to her feet. "We'd best leave the men to manage here." With an arm round her waist she led her back to the inn, but the Irish girl refused to go inside, preferring to remain on the doorstep where she could watch the activity further along the street. Soon the limp figure was bestowed in a farm cart and accompanied by James and some of the men, started the slow process back to the city.

"Let me come," cried Cecilia, darting forward as it passed.

"You'll catch us up on the road," answered her brother and without pausing the little procession passed on out of the village.

"It's all my fault!" exclaimed the fair girl as her aunt came out of the inn, begging for enlightenment.

"Well, come inside while the horses are being put to," suggested Lady

Primrose sensibly, taking in the signs of approaching hysteria, and soon they were seated in the cosy parlour.

"It's all my fault," reiterated Cecilia impatiently, refusing the offered wine.

"I'm sure it was nothing of the kind," said her aunt, comfortably. "Whatever has happened and, so far no-one has told me what that is, I am quite sure it was nothing more than an accident."

She looked enquiringly at Anna, who shook her head and spread her hands in a gesture of bewilderment.

"I bought a cat," began Cecilia, looking out of the window with blank eyes. "A cottage woman brought out the sweetest little kitten and I — I bought it from her." She took a shuddering breath before going on. "It ran away and climbed a tree — I asked Jason Weston to get it for me. He — fell."

"That can hardly be termed your fault. It was very foolish of Ensign Weston to climb a tree, but entirely his own affair if he fell."

Cecilia shot her aunt a hard look, giving a sudden, brittle laugh. "And the funny thing is that the cat got down quite easily. I saw him running away as Jason l-lay on the ground."

Her voice shook and she bit her lip on a sob, turning her face to her friend's shoulder as Anna hastened to comfort her.

"Oh, Anna, Anna," she cried. "I didn't know how much I cared until I s-saw him lying there and thought he was dead! He's always so nice — I know he cared for me, but I've always ignored his feelings — "

Lady Primrose sent her niece a dismayed glance. "I can understand your feelings, my dear, and your sensibility does you justice, but you must remember that Jason Weston's a penniless young man and will remain so even on a sick bed."

Cecilia burst into fresh tears, calling her aunt heartless and Anna was relieved to see the landlord at the door with the news that the coach and horses were waiting.

Rejecting all thought of riding with Lady Primrose, Cecilia mounted her horse, electing Anna to the role of confidante and filling her ears with lamentations on the way home.

Catching up with the wagon and sick man near Knightsbridge, Cecilia would have ridden beside the cortège, until her impatient brother pointed out the impropriety of such an action.

"We had much better go on," said Anna, sensibly taking her bridle, "for it's quite plain that we are only holding up the progress of the cart. The lane is really much too narrow for you to ride abreast. The sooner we go ahead and clear the way, the sooner Mr Weston will be safe in his own bed under the care of a doctor."

Cecilia could not but agree with this and allowed herself to be led ahead, contenting herself with many backward glances until the little procession was lost to view.

"I suppose you must think me very foolish," she said, later that evening.

James not having returned an enquiry had been sent to Standish Square where Ensign Weston had his lodgings, and the two girls were awaiting the reply in Cecilia's bedchamber. Now she suddenly turned away from her anxious watching of the street below and with her back to the long window, went on quickly before Anna could reply.

"You see Jason is so ordinary — not like a hero from romance, and I was so used to having him around," she said, speaking in staccato bursts. "He's always there — always where I want him to be. He is kind and dependable that — I forgot to notice him and just accepted his presence. It wasn't until I saw him lying so still and p-pale that I suddenly realised what life would be like without him." She hung her head and spoke in a small voice. "I — find the thought unbearable."

"Depend upon it, he is suffering no more than a concussion," said Anna, trying to cheer her friend. "Try not to worry. I know he's fond of you and would not wish you to upset yourself on his behalf."

"I wish I'd been kinder to him," sighed the Irish girl, returning to her vigil by the window.

"I'm sure you were never *unkind* — "

"I was — I was. But I've learned my lesson."

Anna looked across the room, noting the determination on the blonde girl's pretty face and remembered Lady Primrose's words. "Your aunt — " she began but was cut short by a fierce gesture from Cecilia.

"I know I am an heiress in a small way and Jason Weston is a poor man, but anyone less like a fortune-hunter is hard to imagine. My money is my own — willed to me by my grandmother. It comes to me when I am of age, whomever I marry." She looked at Anna and smiled. "Faith, I'd be happy on his soldier's pay," she declared, "if only he's suffered no ill effects."

With silent sympathy and understanding Anna put her arm round the other's shoulders and together they watched the street.

"There's that urchin friend of yours," said Cecilia idly, pointing to the doorway opposite. "He always seems to be around lately. I believe he lives on that doorstep."

"I expect you just happen to have noticed him," Anna said and was thankful when the hurrying figure of Betty drove all thought of Ben Bow from the Irish girl's mind.

With a flurry of skirts she ran from the room, her high heels tapping on the polished boards as she hurried to meet her maid. As James had thought, the young soldier's arm was broken, but he had regained consciousness and seemed to have sustained no other hurt. Cecilia was almost delirious with relief and refrained by the impropriety of the action from hurrying to his lodgings and nursing the invalid with her own hands, contented herself by sending messages and sickroom concoctions until Betty declared she had worn a pathway between Standish Square and Essex Street.

A ball to which they had all been looking forward was to be held a few days later and, while at first Cecilia refused all thought of attending, upon hearing that Jason was better she allowed herself to listen to Lady Primrose's blandishments and at last agreed to go.

"Though to be sure I cannot be expected to *enjoy* myself," she announced in the coach as they drove to the home of Sir John and Lady Sligh.

"Of course not," agreed Anna. "I daresay you will not stand up for one dance, but mope in the most interesting manner, filling everyone with curiosity."

James, who was accompanying them snorted with laughter. "Cessy, my love," he said lazily, "you'd best remember, before you go into a decline and wear your heart so plainly upon your sleeve, that Jason has not declared himself yet."

"He has made his feelings very plain," said his sister, tossing her head. "A woman knows when a gentleman cares for her. There are a hundred ways — a touch of the hand, a look . . . a readiness to give aid when needed and before it is asked." She turned to her friend in the corner beside her. "Anna knows, don't you Anna?" she asked.

The other started and turned rather wide eyes in her direction. "I — am not sure. I suppose I do."

The Irish girl's words had started a decidedly disturbing train of thoughts in her mind and she was relieved when they arrived outside the Sligh's house, and she must put her thoughts away and concentrate upon the business of greeting her hosts and saying all that was right and proper as they entered the ballroom and looked round for Lady Primrose who had gone ahead in a sedan-chair.

Having had several daughters to launch upon the world, Lady Sligh had persuaded her husband of the good sense of building a ballroom onto the house and now was the envy of most of the aspiring mothers present.

Anna was struck by a blaze of crystal chandeliers, shining upon gilt and bright chinese wallpaper. They had arrived fashionably late and couples were already forming up for the country dances that were to begin the ball. Lady Primrose, who was deep in conversation with another lady, waved to them to join the dancers and Anna found herself on the end of a row with James for partner while Cecilia was swept away on the arm of an acquaintance.

Usually Anna enjoyed no occupation more than dancing, but tonight her thoughts were elsewhere and her feet followed the measure automatically, while her mind was busy with an astonishing speculation; one that puzzled and dismayed her and one that she refused to allow herself to accept.

Suddenly James' hand tightened on hers and she looked up as he hesitated in the middle of a movement of the dance. Something in the set of his shoulders stilled the question on her lips and following his gaze, she saw a stranger in the entrance, by his stance, obviously searching for someone. His eyes alighted on James and while the pause as he turned his head was almost imperceptible, Anna knew instinctively that a message had been sent and understood.

"Pray excuse me," James murmured, scarcely giving her his attention and leading her perfunctorily to the edge of the dance floor, left her to make her own way to her seat, while he crossed the crowded floor and was soon lost among the kaleidoscope of dancers.

Lady Primrose hardly looked up as the girl seated herself and Anna listened vaguely to the conversation being carried on beside her. Gathering that the topic was an ancient scandal of the ladies' youth, she lost all interest and turned her attention to the people around her, deliberately closing her mind to the thoughts that were uppermost.

A familiar figure approached and bowing to the older woman, begged leave to dance with their companion. Standing up Anna laid her fingers lightly on Captain Bellamy's arm and allowed him to lead her back to the dancers, while her heart pounded so loudly that she half suspected it must be clearly audible to the man beside her.

Resolutely keeping her eyes lowered, she trod the steps in time to the music and refused to meet his gaze.

"Nothing to say, Anna?" he asked quietly, bending his head towards her ear as they met in the pattern of the dance.

"N-no."

Holding her hand, he led her down the line of dancers. "You haven't stammered in a long time," he said softly. "One would suppose you to be particularly nervous tonight."

Her eyes flew to his face above her shoulder as she missed a step, biting her lip in consternation.

"Shall we sit out?" he asked, and

without waiting for her reply, led her out of the dance, through heavy curtains left conveniently open and into the dark garden beyond.

"Oh, please — we should not. People will notice," cried Anna, betraying her agitation.

"Not for a while," assured her companion, leading her to a seat beneath the shadow of a spreading tree and seating himself beside her.

"You are worried — upset. Tell me why."

Anna's hands fluttered as she made a little gesture and suddenly her hands were taken and held in a warm grip, increasing her discomfort.

"I — am a little upset," she confessed, seizing upon the first thing that came to mind to explain her nervousness. "We went to the country for the day and — Jason Weston had an accident."

He studied her carefully, before remarking that he had not supposed her to care so much for the soldier's well-being.

"It's not that," Anna answered impatiently, "'though to be sure, Mr

Weston is a very amiable person, but Cessy has decided she is in love with him — "

"I see, but not why that should bother you."

Anna looked away, wishing she had chosen some other reason for her unease, as the conversation drove her thoughts in a direction she would rather leave alone. "No neither can I," she said, contriving a light laugh and shaking out her fan. "Let us put it down to the weather, there is thunder in the air."

Inconsequently she began to chatter about the recent excursion, until she was brought up short by a sharp enquiry from her companion.

"Walkinshaw did you say?" he asked, a barely concealed excitement in his voice.

"Yes, two sisters, Catherine and Clementina."

His pale eyes gleamed in the moonlight. "Now this is interesting! Clementina, we know, is involved with His Highness — she soothed his fevered brow when he was ill during the Scottish Rebellion, but her sister has always kept clear of the Jacobites."

"Jason said she was a Lady of the Bedchamber to the Princess of Wales."

"Precisely! Things, my dear Anna, are coming to a head. I'll lay wager that messages are flying back and forth at this very minute."

Anna's thoughts involuntarily flew to James' somewhat precipitant exit and reading her expression aright, Captain Bellamy nodded.

"I thought so," he said softly and sat looking at her for long enough to make Anna grow uneasy under his gaze. "I would to God that you were out of it," he said, under his breath, "for now things will become dangerous."

Anna took a little shaken breath and played with the fragile sticks of her fan. "You, sir, were the one to set me on this path," she reminded him.

The fan was removed from her grasp and warm fingers covered her own. "Will you — *can* you forgive me for that?"

Growing very still Anna stole a glance at the soldier's face and found herself unable to read his expression in the dim light of the moon. As he carried her hands to his mouth, the music and conversation

235

in the ballroom behind seemed to fade until she could have been alone in the world with Rafe Bellamy, but as his lips touched her fingers, reminding her forcibly of the other mouth that had kissed her so recently, she started out of the spell that held her and tried to snatch her hands away.

"No!" she cried, struggling to release herself.

At once her hands were dropped, but his grip moved to her shoulders, his fingers biting as he held her. "My dear Anna," he said his voice soft. "I don't believe that is what you said to that Jacobite rogue you're so fond of."

For a moment his eyes gleamed above her and then his fingers tangled in the hair on the nape of her neck and his mouth closed over hers. Anna was too shocked and surprised to move at first, but then she stirred and fought her captor silently. Releasing her as suddenly as he had seized her, Captain Bellamy leaned back a little, regarding her with a slight smile on his mouth.

The icy indifference in his grey eyes, infuriated Anna and dragging the back of her hand across her mouth as though to wipe away the indignity of his kiss, she continued the gesture and struck out at the face above her.

"How d-dare you — I hate you," she cried her voice shaking with suppressed tears.

Catching her wrist, the soldier held it a moment, letting her feel the strength in his slim fingers before he released her contemptuously, almost throwing her hand into her lap.

"I believe you do," he said coldly.

Covering her face with her hands, Anna turned away, trying to hide her distress from his gaze. "Let me go," she begged. "*Please* let me go. How can you make me go on spying for you when you know how I feel? You are — cruel and indifferent. If I could k-kill you I would!"

Her ill-considered words hung in the air between them as the silence grew and at last she recovered her composure enough to sit up and brush away her tears. The man beside her sat like a statue and after a while she was forced to steal a glance at him.

His face appeared pale and hard in a shaft of light spilling out from the curtains behind them. His expression frightened her and it was all she could do not to shrink back as he took a breath.

"Very well," he said, his voice cold and clear. "You are free — I have done with you."

Amazed, Anna stared up at him, her lips slightly parted. "Free," she stammered. "I don't understand. What of Kit?"

Captain Bellamy shrugged. "I'll send his bills to him in the morning, though, I suspect he might want to keep up the acquaintance."

Anna pressed her hands to her eyes. "Do you mean it?" she asked.

"Yes."

"But why — I've asked so often . . . "

"Besotted as you are, you are no use to me." His eyes travelled over her and she flinched from the contempt in his gaze. "You remind me of a love-sick tavern wench, with no thought in her head save the object of her devotion, however unworthy that person may be. I've done with you, Miss Stanton, you may go to the Devil with whom you wish."

Anna bit back a sob. "You are unfair — "

"Am I? I wonder." Standing up, he pulled her to her feet, showing his teeth in a grim smile as he felt her strain away from his nearness. "Pray take my arm, mistress," he said, formally, pulling her fingers through the crook of his elbow. "We must return to the dance — else people remark our absence."

"I can't — they will see," her whisper was agitated and she tried to restore some normality to her appearance with her one free hand.

Tipping up her chin and turning her face to the light, Captain Bellamy took out a handkerchief and wiped away the tears that had gathered under her eyes. For a moment he looked down at her, before returning the linen square to his pocket he took her arm again and led her towards the open window. "Smile," he commanded, as they stepped across the threshold and, blinded by the brilliant candelabras Anna did her best to obey him.

That night Anna lay in bed, listening to the Night Watchman calling the hours and told herself that at last she had what she wanted; freedom from the influence of Captain Bellamy, with Kit safe and herself free to advance her relationship with James in any way she wished without the clouds of guilt she had felt all those months. Restlessly she plumped the pillows and wondered why she should feel far from happy. Pondering miserably on the fact that the thought of the days ahead, far from filling her with joy, seemed dull and empty she at last fell asleep as the first pale rays of the new day crept in at her window.

9

WHEN she was awoken a few hours later by the entry of the maid with a mug of hot chocolate Anna could sense almost at once an air of expectancy that seemed to hang over the house, and when she left her room sometime later to find Cecilia, she was surprised to be met by a general sense of activity as the servants bustled about, carrying sheets and brushes and pails as they made the best chamber ready for a new arrival.

Avoiding a diminutive maid hidden behind a pile of linen, Anna went in search of the Irish girl, tracking her down by following the tinkling notes of the harpsichord to be heard above the more mundane sounds of work.

"Do you expect a visitor?" she asked pleasantly, entering the music room.

Cecilia looked up, taking her fingers from the ivory keys and smiled, mysteriously. "I'll let Aunt Anne tell you herself," she said.

Concealing her curiosity as best she could Anna busied herself tidying the music spread out on a nearby table. "Is it someone interesting?"

"A gentleman from the Continent, I believe," supplied the other girl and obviously not wishing to answer further questions, turned back to the keyboard. "Did you enjoy yourself last night?" she asked. "I thought you looked a little pale. I hope James leaving suddenly didn't upset you — he can be a little lacking in consideration." As Anna shook her head, Cessy improvised, running her fingers across the notes. "Do you like Captain Bellamy?" she asked thoughtfully.

Anna hesitated, realising that the other must have seen her with the soldier and that to dissemble would be foolish. "I think I dislike him," she answered. "He is hard and cold and arrogant."

"Faith!" exclaimed Cecilia, amused. "And what has that red-headed gentleman done to upset you so?"

"N-nothing," muttered Anna, realising some other explanation was called for as her friend raised her eyebrows enquiringly.

"I — believe he led Kit into gambling deeper than he should."

"Your brother is a big boy and old enough to look after himself."

Frowning, Anna recalled how young he had been a few months ago, not in age but in experience and would have told the other so, had Lady Primrose not entered at that moment.

"My dears, my dears," she cried extravagantly, flinging her arms wide as she sank into a chair. "I vow I am worn out and it's not yet noon, such excitement, such comings and goings! So much to be arranged."

"I gather you are expecting a visitor," said Anna quietly.

Lady Primrose and her niece exchanged glances.

"I have left it to you," said Cecilia, meaningly and Lady Primrose moved her gaze to the other girl.

Abruptly, she held out her hand and as Anna took it, drew her to her side. "I understand from James that you are one of us," she said, studying her earnestly, going on as Anna nodded. "Then I charge you, to remember the affection

243

James tells me you bear him and mention what I tell you to no-one."

Taking the girl's silence for agreement the older woman went on. "We *are* expecting a visitor — one of the utmost import — one to whom we all owe allegiance. I am sure I need speak no plainer."

"The Pr — he's coming *here*?" exclaimed Anna. "To London! But surely it's dangerous."

"One in his position does not consider the danger. When a throne is at stake men will venture their all."

"Do you know when to expect him, Aunt?"

Lady Primrose shook her head. "He is at Antwerp, that is all I know. Doubtless tides and ships must be taken into consideration."

"James?" asked Anna, realising that she had not seen him since he had left the ball the previous evening. "Has he gone to meet him?"

"The Prince will travel with his own staff. James has gone to tell our friends of the news and to make sure that the Earl of Westmorland and the Duke of

Beaufort will be in London to meet him."

Suddenly she put a hand to her breast. "Dear God!" she said quietly. "I've waited years for this to happen and now it has . . . I feel in need of my smelling salts!"

"I need hardly tell you girls to mention this to no-one," she said, heaving herself out of the chair. "While the Prince is here, he will be known as Mr Stuart." She smiled slightly. "Not very original, I grant you, but then there must be a good few gentlemen of that name in London and doubtless there is safety in numbers."

"How can he come here, openly like this?" demanded Anna, after dinner that evening, when Lady Primrose and Cecilia had gone into the parlour and she and James were alone momentarily. "It's too dangerous, he'll be caught."

James eyed her enquiringly. "Your loyalty does you credit," he said smoothly, "but take my word for it, the Prince will be as safe here as in Paris. No-one dare touch him."

"I pray you are right," murmured

Anna, remembering Captain Bellamy with a shiver.

Reaching out James tweaked a curl playfully. "Bother yourself with planning entertainments for the Prince and selecting your prettiest gowns to please his eye . . . leave me to see to his safety," he advised and Anna found herself rebelling against his cool delegation of herself to the confines of domesticity.

Possessing himself of her hand, James dropped a kiss into the palm and folded her fingers over it.

"Allow me to worry," he said. "I know your loyalty matches mine, but this is my business, something I have spent years training for."

"It does not seem sensible . . . when so much is in the balance to jeopardize it all when a little care and concealment might make it safe."

Releasing her hand, James swung away, only to turn back and regard her over one shoulder. "Anna," he said slowly, each word pointed and clear. "I fear you do not realise, that only dedicated Jacobites know of his plans, no-one else knows of his proposal to come here, so who could put him in danger? Are you suggesting that one of us would betray him . . . or that a spy is in our midst?"

Avoiding his eyes, Anna idly turned over the pages of a book left open on a table. "No — you are right," she agreed. hoping her voice would not betray her inner agitation. "It was foolish of me to worry when you have everything under control."

James shrugged. "It's understandable for you to worry," he said, "but you must learn to take my word for what it is worth and not bother yourself about matters which are my concern."

Anna knew a faint irritation at the note of patronage in his voice but dismissing her mood as due to her late night, turned the conversation to other matters.

"I had a letter from Kit this morning," she said as they left the room to join the others in the parlour. "He tells me his regiment has been ordered North."

"Indeed," James was interested. "Do you know whereabouts?"

"Fort William — I believe it's in the West of Scotland. I'm sorry he is being sent so far, but at least it's better than

America, which is where I feared he might be ordered."

"America would be of little use — but Scotland — well, there's been a rising there, before."

Anna looked up at him, puzzled, as he reached to open the door for her. "I don't understand what you mean," she said, slowly.

James smiled down at her. "Merely that a friend in an enemy camp is always useful."

Realisation of his meaning made Anna open her eyes wide. "Kit would never spy for you," she said positively.

The shoulders under the wine red velvet lifted and fell. "Who can tell?" he wondered lightly. "With a sister of Jacobite convictions, surely he can be expected to listen to her suggestions with a kind ear."

"I'd never ask him to betray his — "

James' finger touched her lips, silencing the flood of words. "Ssh — don't be so vehement, my dearest Anna. It was only a suggestion. Something for the future." He smiled down at her and took his finger away. "What a bundle of confusion you are — sometimes I think you forget that you are loyal to the Stuarts!"

"At first it was only fun — like play acting," she said, ingenuously. "It's only since I've known you and realised what you were trying to do that my loyalties have become certain and even now I still forget occasionally."

James laughed and reached forward to drop a light kiss on her mouth. "Spoken like a true female," he said, teasingly. "I believe that given the wish and the opportunity, I could make a true Hanoverian of you!"

Opening the door and sweeping her into the room, he did not see Anna's confusion and going to the window she was able to regain her composure before anyone noticed her embarrassment.

The household lived in a turmoil of expectancy for the next few days, expecting the imminent arrival of the Prince, however when he did arrive in the middle of September it was at a most inopportune moment: Lady Primrose had decided to give a card party and, whether out of bravado or boredom, had invited several known Whigs to make up the numbers, including Captain Bellamy.

Anna, who was crossing the hall at the time, saw a tall, slightly plump, fair headed man waiting silently, while his companion spoke to the butler and meeting his eyes, dropped a small curtsey.

"Mr Stuart, at your service," he said, with the suspicion of an accent, tossing back the heavy folds of his travelling cloak to make her a bow.

Eyes wide, Anna stared at him in silence, before recovering her wits, she hastily closed the door on the card party. "Y-you are expected, Sir," she said, making a more elaborate genuflection, "but I fear the house is full of Whigs."

The Prince's eyebrows raised. "Did you hear that, Brett?" he asked the man behind him. "A reception committee awaits me."

"No-no, nothing like that — just a card party," Anna made haste to assure him, gesturing to the butler to fetch James. "If you will follow me, Mr Drelincourt will be with you in a minute."

And turning on her heel, she led the way to the library at the back of the house. Seeing the Prince's companion glancing around, she pointed out the garden door to him.

"I like a means of escape," he said simply, opening the door to glance briefly into the garden, before joining the Prince in the library.

Closing the door on them, Anna saw James come into the hall and hurried to meet him.

"I've put them in the library," she told him. "I thought it best — I didn't know where — "

He nodded, patted her on the shoulder and shut himself into the small room with the new arrivals. Anna stared at the closed door, listening to the murmur of voices behind its thick boards, for a moment, before returning to the card party.

"Was that someone?" asked Lady Primrose, looking up from her hand of cards as Anna entered.

"S–someone for James," Anna said, thinking it better for Lady Primrose to be in ignorance for the moment, and passed on to seat herself near a window, while waiting to be called to make up a game.

Once seated, she glanced round the room, with an assumption of idleness but in reality to assure herself that no-one had given undue attention to the newcomers. Across the room, she met the steady gaze of Rafe Bellamy and felt her heart turn over as his eyes travelled thoughtfully from her to the hall door knowing with dreadful certainty that his interest was obviously aroused.

Realising that she must allay his suspicions, she stood up on trembling legs and went to join him, with an air of ease she was in reality far from feeling.

"Poor James," she said lightly, hovering over the table at which he was playing, "to be called away on business in the middle of a game."

The other players made sympathetic murmurs, but Captain Bellamy put his fan of cards face down on the table and placing his fingers lightly over them smiled up at her.

"Business, is it?" he queried. "I thought it must be someone of much more import . . . there almost seemed an air of excitement about Mr Drelincourt as he left the room."

Forcing herself to meet his grey eyes guilelessly, Anna shook her head. "His manager from Ireland," she improvised quickly, remembering the accent of the Prince's companion. "A Colonel Brett, I believe."

For a moment, she thought there was a spark of intense speculation in his eyes, but then the soldier turned away. "No doubt Mr Drelincourt will return when he's able," he said indifferently, and returned his interest to the cards he held and his interrupted game.

Feeling she had done her best, Anna continued round the room, making excuses for James, hiding the nervousness she was feeling under an ease of manner which she was unhappily aware would not deceive the shrewd man behind her.

At last the card party was over, the players gone and the news broken to Lady Primrose of her august guest's arrival. Having recourse to her smelling-bottle, the older lady clutched Anna's hand, but soon regained control and presented herself at the door of the library, leaving Cecilia outside, agog and plying Anna with breathless questions.

"What is he like?" she demanded.

Anna wrinkled her forehead. "Very ordinary," she said. "A young man no-one would look twice at — save that he has a certain air about him."

The Irish girl made an impatient noise, snorting inelegantly as she seized her friend's arm and dragged her upstairs, saying that she, for one, was going to put on her best gown and dazzle His Royal Highness at dinner that night, and if Anna had any sense she would do the same.

The Prince declared that he wished for no formality, but his manner was so quiet and remote that the conversation round the long table grew stilted and at last would have ceased altogether but for the gallant efforts of Lady Primrose and soon even she rolled an appealing eye in the direction of her nephew.

At once he was on his feet. "A toast!" he cried, "before the ladies leave us."

Hastily the glasses were refilled and the assembly scrambled to their feet as James lifted his glass.

"I give you His Majesty King James the Third."

The Prince drank with them, before hurling his glass into the fireplace, breaking it so that no other toast could be drunk from it. Anna saw Lady Primrose flinch as her best crystal crashed against the grate, and could not but admire the way in which she hid her dismay as the rest of the company followed suit.

The ladies retired to drink tea and discuss their visitor in discreet tones until the clock in the hall struck midnight and they knew that the men were too deep in intrigue to join them.

"Well, I must say events are not as exciting as I expected," said Cecilia in disgust, as she and Anna mounted the stairs to their bedchambers.

"And a good thing, too," replied the other girl, repressing a shudder. "I shall be glad when he's gone again."

"What do you think he's come for?" wondered Cecilia.

"I've no idea — we must ask James."

But James was unusually tight mouthed on that point and try as she would, Anna was still as ignorant a few days later. The Prince appeared to behave much as any man on holiday; he visited the Tower and apparently discussed with Colonel Brett, who accompanied him everywhere, how best to seize it. He viewed St James' Palace, where the Hanoverian King held Court, was received into the Anglican Church, a move which would make easier his acceptance as future King of a Protestant people, who by tradition and inclination were wary of Catholics, and met many of his followers in a room in Pall Mall.

By now Anna had almost decided that he had come to England with no clear action in mind, but suddenly events took a new turn and one that revived her flagging interest.

A message was delivered to the Prince one evening after dinner. He tore it open, read it and thrust it towards his pocket, but in his haste and excitement missed the opening in his coat skirt and dropped the crumpled paper on the floor.

Anna, who was nearest, picked it up and returned it to him, but not before she had glanced quickly at the scrawled lines and read the heading.

Picking up her needlework again she

plied her needle with composure, while turning over the address in her mind. 'Leicester House'. The name was familiar, she was certain she had heard it before and quite recently. Suddenly the illusive memory returned to her and she looked at her companions surreptitiously, wondering if they had heard her indrawn breath of surprise.

Leicester House in Leicester Fields was where the Prince of Wales lived! Stabbing her material with a needle that shook, she wondered at the reason behind any communication between the two Princes of rival houses and despite racking her brains, could come to no satisfactory conclusion, but Captain Bellamy's description of civil war returned vividly to her mind filling her sleep that night with dreams of horror.

She awoke next morning with a growing determination to do her best to prevent such horrors happening again on English soil, finding herself unexpectedly in agreement with the soldier when he had said that no cause was worth the terrible effect it would have.

For once Ben Bow seemed to have

deserted his post in the doorway opposite and Anna was non-plussed as how to get word to the Captain. Pondering her problem, she was wandering deep in thought towards her own room when Cecilia called to her from her bedchamber.

"Come in and close the door," she commanded.

Anna looked at her with interest. "What's the matter?" she demanded. "You're looking very serious."

"Sure, it's not surprising if I am," cried the Irish girl. "Haven't I been trying to persuade my brother to take me to see Jason and when at last he agrees, he changes his mind at the last moment!"

"Does Lady Primrose not object to the scheme?"

"Don't be silly, she has no idea of the affair at all." Cecilia flung herself down in front of her dressing-table and stared moodily at her reflection in the mirror. "And that's not all — having withdrawn his presence my precious brother demands that Betty, instead of accompanying me in his place, must stay

258

here in order to carry a letter from the Prince."

"*Betty*," exclaimed Anna, her eyes going to the small figure, busy with folding linen.

"Yes, Betty — sure and can you imagine anyone less like a spy to carry messages? Whatever you're doing getting yourself involved in intrigue, I can't imagine," she went on to her maid, "but let me tell you, it doesn't endear you to me at all."

"I'm sorry, miss," cried the girl, "but when Mr James told me to, I could not say no."

"You should have come to me," said her mistress severely, ignoring a doleful sniff and turning to Anna. "Now Anna. I'm relying on you for some way out of this dilemma, for I am determined to see Jason this afternoon."

"Lady Primrose would hardly think it proper — "

"Poof to my aunt and her conventions," cried the other girl. "See Jason I will, if I have to go alone."

Anna eyed her friend warily, knowing she was quite capable of carrying out her threat. "I'll come with you," she offered, reluctantly.

"Yes, well . . . that's kind of you, but to tell the truth there's more *convention* in the presence of one's maid and, to be honest, in the circumstances I think it would be better if Betty accompanied me."

"Cessy, my love," laughed Anna, "you make it abundantly clear that you don't want me to play gooseberry, so *what* do you want me to do?"

"Was I as plain as that?" wondered the fair girl ingenuously. "I thought I was quite subtle. I want you to stay here and take Betty's place if James should send her on a message."

Anna's eyes widened. "Me!" she exclaimed. "Oh, Cessy, use your brains — how could you expect James to mistake me for Betty?"

With her head on one side, Cecilia considered her. "You're both dark and about the same size. Wearing one of her gowns and a frilly cap and straw hat on your head, I'm sure you'd pass. Besides we — James never looks at the servants, you know."

Anna was suddenly struck by the possibilities of the proposition before her and sat down abruptly, as her breath caught at the suggestion that the illusive message might be put into her very hands. "A-all r-right," she stammered, hoping the other would not notice her sudden agitation. "I'll do it."

"I knew you would," cried Cecilia, jumping up to throw her arms around her friend. "Now, Betty is to sit in here all afternoon and if the Prince wishes a message taken, the letter will be brought here, which she is to take at once to Leicester House and to ask for a Miss Walkinshaw. Can you remember that?"

"I think so," answered Anna, trying to show no recognition of the name. "Do I just hand it in?"

Cecilia looked inquiringly at her maid who nodded. "What a good, brave girl you are," she said, impulsively. "I vow there never was such a friend."

Suppressing her feelings of guilt, Anna smiled weakly, resolutely putting aside any thoughts of betrayal and treachery that intruded by reminding herself of the holocaust that would follow, should the Stuart Prince succeed in rousing his followers.

Much later, the house was still in the heat of the September afternoon and Anna was sitting alone in the upstairs room, Cecilia and Betty having left on their sick visit. She had drawn the curtains to darken the room, tied the strings of the linen cap tightly under her chin and pulled the wide-brimmed straw hat low over her eyes. Examining herself in the mirror, and seeing the wide eyed servant girl in the plain blue dress that stared back at her she was almost convinced that no-one would recognise her, but when a tap sounded at the door behind her, the sound startlingly loud in the quiet house, her heart jumped and began to pound against her bodice. Keeping her head down, she opened the door, staring at the feet of the person who had knocked.

A sealed, folded paper, was held towards her. "Do you remember your instructions?" asked James. "You are to take this to Leicester House and give it to Miss Walkinshaw."

Anna nodded and taking the letter, dropped a servant's bob, as a gold coin was slipped into her hand.

"Another for you when you return," James said easily, turning away.

Watching his retreating back, Anna reflected how easy it had been, realising for the first time with what indifference and lack of interest the lower orders were treated in aristocratic society.

Earlier, peering from the window, she had been relieved to see that Ben was back at his post and going to the window she attracted his attention and made signs for him to meet her at the back of the house.

Avoiding the servants, she slipped out of the garden, finding Ben beside her as she closed the narrow door in the high wall.

"Coo, miss, you don't half look different," he exclaimed. "I wasn't sure it was you."

"I must see Captain Bellamy," Anna told him. "Can you take me to him?"

The boy eyed her uncertainly. "I thought as you weren't working for him any more?"

"Then why were you still watching the house?"

Shrugging his thin shoulders, Ben thrust both hands into the pockets of his tattered breeches. "'Cos he told me to," he said simply.

Shaking one thin arm impatiently, Anna showed him the guinea so recently bestowed upon herself. "You can have this," she said enticingly.

Ben's eyes widened and he made to snatch the coin from her hands, but she held it out of his reach with a quick movement. "*After* I've seen the Captain."

"Come on, then," the child commanded, taking her hand, "but I don't know he'll be there."

Leading her through the streets, Anna realised that they were heading towards the river and much sooner than she had anticipated, Ben stopped outside a tall, elegant house.

"Second floor, miss," he said, holding out his hand, turning on his heels at once, as Anna dropped the money into his grubby palm.

For a moment Anna stood looking up at the narrow building, noting the shining brass door knocker and gleaming paintwork; obviously Rafe Bellamy lived in the first degree of elegance and luxury. Gathering her wilting courage, she mounted the whitened steps and lifting the heavy lion's head, knocked at the door.

A small, elderly man, with the air of a retired gentleman's valet opened the door and regarded her inquiringly.

"C-Captain Bellamy. Is he within? I have a message for him."

The man's eyes travelled over her, taking in the servant's attire and obviously puzzled by its variance with her speech.

"I'll see," he said reluctantly, at last. "What name?"

"Stanton," supplied Anna and was left on the step in front of the closed door, while the man went in search of the soldier.

Feeling conspicuous, Anna examined the street, trying to appear as if she was used to waiting on doorsteps and was inordinately grateful when the door was opened again, and she was invited inside.

Rafe Bellamy turned from the window as she was shown into his room and lifted his eyebrows.

"Fancy dress, Miss Stanton?" he

murmured, taking in her unusual costume."

Shrugging aside his sally, Anna spoke quietly. "I have news of great import — " she began, but the man opposite turned away and reseated himself at the desk he had vacated on her entrance.

His attitude, while she still stood was a studied insult, but choosing to ignore his actions Anna hurried on.

"The Prince is with us, as you no doubt know."

"Indeed, I do," Rafe Bellamy interrupted again, "but I am at a loss as to why you should feel obliged to inform me of the fact."

"I scarce know myself," Anna confessed, candidly "unless your tales of civil war have borne fruit. Whatever the cause I think you'd be wise to listen to me."

Narrowed grey eyes held hers for a long minute, before she was gestured to a chair.

"The Prince has received a letter from Leicester House," she told him without preamble.

"The Devil he has!" exclaimed the Captain.

"And what is more, has sent a reply."

"Do you know what was in them?"

At her shake of the head, Captain Bellamy's fingers beat an impatient tattoo on his desk top and after a minute, Anna could retain her moment of triumph no longer.

"But I have it here with me!" she burst out.

His expression incredulous, the man opposite regarded her blankly, reaching out slowly to take the letter she produced from her skirt pocket.

Lighting a candle, he held a knife in its flame before sliding the hot blade under the black seal and straightening out the heavy, folded paper. Quickly he read the few lines of writing and looked up.

"I take it, Miss Stanton, that we are working together again," he said quietly.

"In this instance," said Anna slowly, avoiding his gaze. "I find I do not care for rebellion."

"Then we have one goal in mind." Hastily resealing the letter, he pushed it across the desk towards her. "Take it, Anna, and deliver it as you were told.

Then go home and forget you took this detour to me."

"But — what does it say?"

"It's best that you don't know. Your Jacobites are dangerous men. If you let slip your knowledge they would want to know how you received it."

As she slipped the letter into the safety of her pocket, hidden in the blue folds of her skirt, the man behind the desk stood up and went to hold the door for her.

"My thanks," he said, simply as she paused on the threshold and, impulsively, Anna held out her hand.

His grasp was firm and warm as he took her fingers, not shaking her hand as she intended but holding it for a moment, before carrying it to his lips.

Above her hand, their eyes met and held, something in his expression making Anna catch her breath, as she looked away.

"I m-must go!" she stammered, snatching away her hand and almost ran from the house.

To her relief Ben Bow was waiting in the street with a sedan-chair he had procured for her. Climbing in, she thanked him for his help and dismissed him. Seeming to think she needed his presence, he was prepared to argue, but as the chair was lifted and the men started forward, Anna waved him away and rather reluctantly, he obeyed her, standing forlornly on the street as she was carried away.

Anna asked to be taken to the back of Leicester House, judging that there her servant's costume would be less likely to attract attention and in a surprisingly short time, her chair was set down at the back entrance of the old Tudor building. Scarcely sparing a glance for the red brick and low mullioned windows, Anna hurried inside. No-one in the busy kitchens took any notice of her and she realised what a perfect disguise was her borrowed blue gown and tapping a small boy on the arm, asked for Miss Walkinshaw.

Without a word the child took her arm and led her through countless corridors and rooms until they were in a less frequented part of the house and left her in front of a low door. Looking after his retreating back, Anna swallowed her feelings of desertion and plucking up her courage tapped timidly on the wooden panels darkened by age.

The door was opened by a middle-aged woman, who stared at the intruder inquiringly.

"M-miss Walkinshaw?" asked Anna and was shown into the room, with such lack of surprise that she knew a visitor had been expected.

One of the two women who had been at the outing to Kensington came forward, holding out an imperious hand and remembering to curtsey, Anna dropped the letter into her waiting palm.

"Wait," commanded Miss Walkinshaw and sailed from the room with a rustle of silk skirts.

The older woman took up a position in front of the empty fireplace, her hands neatly folded, her eyes fastened on Anna. The wait under the steady gaze seemed interminable and Anna shuffled uneasily from foot to foot, trying to hide her growing nervousness. At last the Princess' bed-woman reappeared, thrust the note she carried into the waiting girl's hands and enjoined her to deliver it to no-one but Mr Stuart, himself.

Quite suddenly, it seemed to Anna, she found herself in the dark corridor, the door firmly closed behind her and the prospect of finding her own way out of the labyrinth-like house. Rounding the first corner she almost fell over the child she had accosted in the kitchens, who appeared to be waiting for her, as he took her hand again and set off at a furious pace.

Dusk was falling as she pushed open the heavy outer door and it was with relief that she saw that the chair-men were still waiting for her. Climbing wearily into the cramped interior of the sedan, she gave Lady Primrose's address and sank back as the door was closed on her, only to start up again as she remembered to ask to be set down at the garden entrance.

Quietly entering the house, she listened to the soft murmur of voices from behind the library door, before rapping her knuckles against the wood. The door was opened at once, as though someone had waited on the other side and seeing whom it was James held out his hand imperiously. Thankful that her errand was over, Anna gave him the folded paper and without waiting hurried upstairs to her room.

Flinging off the wide-brimmed hat, she sank down on the bed and kicked off her shoes, just as the door opened and Cecilia entered.

"He's up and about," she declared, intent only on one thing and expecting her friend to share her interest. "We found him in his parlour, with his arm in a sling and a vile bruise upon his head, poor fellow. I must say he seemed to brighten when I entered and I am sure we left him in better spirits." She eyed the other girl doubtfully for a moment, before obviously making up her mind, and going on, "I will tell you, Anna, for I am sure you will be discreet, that we have almost come to an understanding — at least he said there was a lady very dear to him, to whom he only refrained from declaring himself due to the fact that she was an heiress and himself almost penniless. Oh, Anna, it must be me, don't you think?"

"Sure to be," agreed Anna, raising one hand to her aching head and struck by the singular lack of interest in her news, Cecilia examined her friend with new eyes.

"Are you all right?" she asked. "How did this afternoon go? I vow you're very pale — you're not ill?"

"Only tired — I've not walked so far, since I left the country."

"Whyever didn't you take a chair?"

"I did — after a while, but it wasn't the streets that wore me out, it was Leicester House, it's a maze of passages and corridors. I must have walked miles ... dragged along by some child of about nine or ten, at a pace better suited to one of the Greek runners of old, than a modern young lady!" She groaned feelingly and wriggled her toes.

Cecilia murmured sympathetically and returned to her more interesting subject, leaving Anna only when it was time to dress for dinner.

The meal that evening was an odd affair: the men were charged with suppressed excitement, Lady Primrose, who seemed totally unaware of the atmosphere chatted on inconsequently, in her best hostess manner, while Cecilia was quiet and restrained still with the wounded Jason in her thoughts. Only Anna was aware of the hidden feelings of the men as they ate their meal and conversed amicably.

The Prince was less constrained than usual, his fair skin glowing brightly with excitement. When the meal was over and Lady Primrose gave the signal for the ladies to retire and leave the men to their port, he stayed her with a gesture and stood up, his blue satin coat shining in the light from

"Pray stay a moment," he said. "Having enjoyed your hospitality and kindness I feel it only right that you should know that I expect a happy outcome to my journey."

"Your Highness — " warned James, leaning forward, but the Prince hushed him with a movement of his hand.

"You yourself have told me, my dear Drelincourt, that only the most loyal of Jacobites dwell under your roof, therefore what have I to fear in telling your aunt and these young ladies, that a meeting has been arranged between Frederick of Hanover and I — and that we intend to come to a settlement whereby Prince Frederick will rule over the dominions and I shall be King of the British Isles."

His voice rang triumphantly around the table as he gazed about him, his eyes bright with fulfilled hope and exaltation. Anna caught her breath as she realised what had been in the letter she had carried . . . and with the realisation came a new knowledge. Her heart began to beat so loudly, that it drowned the sounds of the excited conversation around her and she clutched the edge of the table for fear that she would fall.

The Prince smiled at the company and bowed. "And now I must leave you — I go to meet my kinsman from Hanover."

He had reached the door, before Anna had recovered enough to move. Tipping over her skirts she darted forward.

"D-don't go," she cried, clutching his sleeve in her agitation. "You must not go!"

10

THE Prince did not brush Anna's hand away, but stiffened at her touch, staring at her with so cold an air and so remotely, that her hand fell away from his blue sleeve and she hung her head, praying desperately that the last few minutes had been a dream and that she would wake to find herself safe in bed.

"I do not understand," said the Prince coldly. "If you are concerned for my safety, I assure you that Colonel Brett and Mr Drelincourt will take good care of me."

A hand took hold of her elbow, nipping unkindly as she was drawn away from the door and turned to face the room.

"I think you had best explain yourself," said James, quietly, his blue eyes ice-cold and sharp with speculation as he searched her face.

One glance at his closed expression was enough to fill Anna with dismay at the enormity of what she must confess and losing her courage she sought desperately for a way out.

"I — was afraid for His Highness," she said lamely, and knew as she said it, that she would not be believed.

"Aunt Anne, will you and Cecilia leave us?" James said in almost a conversational tone and waited silently until the two women had left the room with many puzzled, backward glances.

"Now, Anna," he said, as the door closed behind them, "the truth if you please."

Swallowing, Anna felt herself begin to tremble, knowing that the tale she must tell, would strain James' affection for her to its limits. Several times she tried to begin, but the task was so difficult and made more so by the three pairs of eyes which watched her, that she bit her lip and shook her head.

"We are waiting," said James into the silence.

And at last, casting away all caution Anna told them the whole story. At first her voice shook, but as she proceeded, emboldened by the listeners' silence, it grew stronger until, when she had finished her words seemed to hang in the air.

The Prince was the first to speak. "What is this?" he demanded, staring from one to the other. "I do not understand. Am I to believe that she is a spy?"

"I am afraid so," said James, his eyes fixed on the girl, his face unusually pale and tense.

"Then — all my plans are known to this Captain Bellamy — this Whig spy?"

There was so much despair in the Prince's voice that, involuntarily, Anna's eyes flew to his face, seeing a man who was confronted by the death of all his dreams. Knowing that he had lost that which had almost been within his grasp, Charles Edward Stuart turned away, leaning over the table so that his face was in shadow, but his shaking hands and bowed shoulders spoke eloquently of his emotions.

At that moment Anna would have given her life to remove the result of her actions. "I had to," she cried, trying to justify what she had done. "Don't you see — if the Prince raises his standard in England there can only be civil war."

"So the Usurper Hanover is to be tolerated, merely because a few lives might be lost — "

"We are wasting time," Colonel Brett cut across James furious words. "Your Highness, we must decide what to do."

"I have arranged to meet Prince Frederick and I intend to do so."

"Without a doubt the meeting place will be surrounded, if you are not intercepted on the way. Soldiers may even now be on the way here."

The Prince sighed and stood up, making a helpless gesture as he turned back into the room. "What do you suggest, Brett, my friend?" he asked wearily, his accent much in evidence.

"With your leave, Sir — I would suggest that you leave here immediately, with luck you could be on a ship and at sea by morning. An attempt must be made to get a warning to Leicester House." His eyes travelled to James.

"That shall be my task," he offered at once, eager to make amends for Anna's betrayal.

Colonel Brett nodded, his eyes travelling onto Anna. "The girl must be taken care of," he pointed out matter of factly.

"No harm must come to her," put in the Prince. "Whatever her convictions and however misguided, she is still one of my subjects. I will not have her hurt."

"No, Your Highness," murmured Colonel Brett, his eyes meeting James significantly behind the Prince's back, as he dropped a phial discreetly into the younger man's hand.

"Th-thank you, Your Highness," stammered Anna, dropping into a deep curtsey. "I — am truly sorry — "

Prince Charles gave a wintry smile. "Not more so than I," he said softly and allowed himself to be hurried from the room by his aide. "J-James," faltered Anna as the door closed behind them and was met by a glance of such furious disgust, that her supplicating hand fell back to her side and she stared in dismay.

"You conniving doxy!" he snarled. "Somehow you have managed to ruin all our plans, years of effort and organization have been put at naught . . . and all by you!" Incredulity raged in his voice. "I would not have believed it."

"F-forgive me," she pleaded, touching his arm.

Throwing off her hand with an impatient gesture, he went to the table and poured wine into a glass, splashing red liquid onto the polished wood. Uncorking the phial, he tipped its contents into the glass and came back to the girl.

"James," said Anna, searching his face, "cannot you understand and forgive me? I would try to understand your motives if you did something distasteful to me."

"Indeed," he snorted derisively. "How noble!"

"No, not noble, because I have a-affection for you," she said as steadily as she was able. "Don't you care for me at all? Do our words and moments together mean nothing?"

James laughed and one look at his face as he approached told her the shattering truth.

"Nothing at all," he told her cruelly, each word sharp and clear. "You are very foolish, Anna my dear, if you believe that I ever cared a fig for you. You were available — and to have you besotted by me would ensure your loyalty — "

Suddenly Anna saw the man before her clearly for the first time, his handsome face cruel and hard and realised that he was more ruthless and indifferent to anyone who stepped in his way, than Rafe Bellamy ever was and with the knowledge came a return of her courage.

Drawing herself up, she faced her adversary with dignity. "But it didn't, did it James?" she pointed out calmly. "And if you think I am going to drink the wine you have just doctored, you are quite mistaken."

James' eyes flickered at the change in her, but he still advanced towards her, making her slowly back away. "No-one will come to your aid," he told her, softly, his voice holding a hint of amusement and with a plunge of her heart, she realised that he was enjoying the situation. "I am stronger than you . . . and if necessary I shall forget I am a gentleman."

"Were you ever?" she wondered and found herself trapped between the wall and a heavy sideboard.

"I'm afraid society has put a veneer on me," he smiled, his eyes very bright as he realised his quarry was cornered. "And now, Anna, what are you going to do?"

Wildly she looked round for means of escape, her eyes at last having to come back to his pitiless face. Little Devils were dancing in his eyes and suddenly her nerve broke and she plunged forward. He had been waiting for such a move and pinned her effortlessly against him with one arm, tipping her head back against his shoulder as he poured the contents of the glass ruthlessly down her throat.

Gasping and choking, Anna was forced to swallow most of the wine even though she fought the man who held her with desperate fear.

"Are you afraid it's poison?" he wondered, amused as he felt the wild beating of her heart. "My poor Anna — there's nothing you can do about it, if it is."

His laugh echoed wildly in Anna's mind as the drug took effect, and as a feeling of horror overwhelmed her, she fell in to a spinning world of enveloping, velvet darkness.

When Anna regained consciousness, it seemed to be day and she lay for a moment wondering what was the red glow she could see, before realising that she lay in her own bed and that a fire burned slowly in the hearth. At her slight movement a woman rose from her seat beside the fire and approached the bed.

"Awake are you, dearie?" she asked in a hoarse voice and Anna shrank back against her pillows as a wave of gin-laden breath washed towards her as the woman bent over her.

"W-who are you?" she asked and was dismayed to find how weak her voice was.

"Lor' love you, missy, I'm your nurse," said the woman, showing a row of blackened stumps as she smiled ingratiatingly.

"Nurse! Am I ill?"

"Your guardian, the good lady, tells me they suspect smallpox — "

Anna stared blankly at her. "I have no guardian — " she began slowly, only to break off abruptly as memory returned to her. Flinging back the bedclothes she sat up. "Neither am I ill," she said in firmer tones, preparing to climb out of bed.

"Now dearie, be a good girl," said the woman in a voice that made Anna look up to find her standing over her. One large, red hand took the girl's shoulder and pressed her back against the pillows, while the covers were drawn up and tucked firmly in. "I was paid to look after you, missy — to keep you in bed and quiet — do you understand?"

"I — think so."

"So long as you do, we'll get along very well. I like a peaceful life myself. You can call me Mrs Rivers, most of my patients do."

Putting aside the ambiguity of her words for the moment, Anna lay back, regarding her silently. One look at the enormous frame and powerful arms told her clearly that she would be no match for the nurse in a trial of strength.

"M-Mrs Rivers," she said tentatively after a while, when the woman had returned to her seat by the fire, "you must realise that I am a prisoner — "

"I don't realise nothing," said Mrs

285

Rivers, not looking up from her task of feeding the fire. "I was paid to take care of you — " She suddenly turned a speculative eye on the girl in bed. "You haven't got more than a pony tucked away in your stocking, I suppose?"

The expression on Anna's face gave her the answer and shrugging, she turned away, while the girl contemplated the fact that Lady Primrose or James were paying this dreadful woman twenty pounds to keep her quiet; so large a sum telling her plainly how determined they were to make sure of her security.

The day passed in enforced idleness, boredom replacing her fear, once she had realised that nothing was planned for her at the moment. Meals were brought to them and half hidden under her plate Anna found a folded scrap of paper. Sliding it under her pillow with a sleight of hand she had not known she possessed, she waited until the other woman had fallen into a doze, before stealthily retrieving it. Each fold seemed to crackle loudly, but at last it was open and she could read the untidy scrawl of Cecilia's hasty writing.

'Aunt Anne says you are too ill for me to see and rather than risk infection she is sending me home, a thought that you must know I cannot contemplate with fortitude, and will realise why I say remember me with kindness —
Your loving friend,
Cessy.'

For a moment Anna stared at the note, her brows knitted in perplexity, before the woman by the fire stirred and she quickly pushed it under her pillow.

Watching the nurse carefully, Anna discovered that she took most of her nourishment from a large, black bottle she kept beside her chair, her face growing steadily redder as the day progressed. Having consumed a large, rich dinner, she sustained herself all evening with sips from her bottle until at last falling heavily asleep sometime after the hall clock had struck midnight.

Pushing back the bedclothes, Anna slipped quietly out of bed. Trying the door she found as she had supposed that it was locked on the outside. Non-plussed she gazed around the over-heated room, until her eyes fell on the window and hurrying across the wooden floor, she pushed aside one heavy curtain and stared out at the dark garden.

Pulling the curtain across behind her, Anna struggled with the heavy latch of the window, releasing it at last enough to raise the sash a foot or two. Kneeling, she peered out, hoping to find some means of escape. A leaden drainpipe passed close by on its journey to a water butt below and reaching out she gave it a tentative shake, wondering if she could trust herself to its somewhat frail, strength.

A movement below caught her attention and drawing back, she crouched on the floor, her heart beating quickly, until the stealthiness of the figure below convinced her that it did not belong to the household. Watching, she saw it dart like a wraith from bush to bush and shadow to shadow, each move bringing it nearer to the terrace below her window. Hanging over the windowsill she stared down at the pale face raised to hers, realising its endearing familiarity.

"Ben, oh Ben!" she breathed, her heart jumping alarmingly.

"They say you've got the pox," he whispered piercingly.

"No — no. I'm not ill . . . They are keeping me prisoner."

Ben stared up at her consideringly. "Can you get out?" he asked. His eyes falling on the drainpipe he shook it vigorously, making it creak ominously, and hang drunkenly away from the wall.

"Shush," cried Anna. "Be quiet, do. There's a woman in my room, and if she should hear — "

"You'd best not try the drainpipe," counselled the boy, giving it a final disgusted shake.

"The door's locked," hissed Anna.

For a moment Ben was at a loss, staring up at her his face a pale blob in the fleeting moonlight. "I'd best be off — " he said reluctantly.

"Don't leave me, Ben," whispered Anna, leaning farther out of the window, but already the small figure was backing across the terrace.

"I'll tell the Captain," his voice floated up to her as he scurried into the shadows, melting into the darkness, until try as she would she could no longer see him.

Shivering in the cold night air, Anna closed the window and relatched it, peering out cautiously from the curtains to make sure the nurse was still asleep, before running across the room and climbing back into bed, burrowing among the blankets for warmth. Tucking her toes into the folds of her nightgown and hugging her arms around herself, Anna tried to still the chattering of her teeth, while thoughts of previous events returned to plague her. During the day she had resolutely put aside all memory of what had happened, but now in the still, lonely and endless night thoughts of James filled her mind and she shed hot, bitter tears.

The dawn found her hot eyed and restless, but at last able to face the fact that he had never cared for her and admitted to herself that what she had felt for him had been far from the true, lasting love she had thought it to be. With bitter reflection she realised that her love for him had been romantic fantasy, based upon a fictitious hero she had invented, rather than the real ruthless, ambitious young Jacobite; and with the knowledge came a renewal of the fear that had beset her all day. Although the Prince had ordered her safety, she knew in her heart that she was too much of a danger to the group of conspirators to ever be allowed free.

With the break of day, the household returned to life, with a renewal of the sounds of hustle and bustle from beyond her locked door. Mrs Rivers started awake at a particularly loud noise from the corridor and Anna asked her curiously what was happening.

"Packing," said the woman, succinctly, straightening her cap and vainly tucking away loosened strands of coarse grey hair. "The furniture is all being put under Holland covers and the plate and clothes packed to be taken back to Ireland."

Anna lay still digesting this, while the woman answered a tap at the door, receiving whispered instructions and a tray of food.

"Good news, dearie," she said, placing the tray across Anna's knees. "You must

291

be better — you're to be up and dressed and ready to receive a visitor this morning."

Ignoring her heavy irony, Anna asked whom her visitor was to be, but received only a disinterested shrug in reply as the woman helped herself to some chops from a dish and taking a mug of beer, retired to the fireside again.

Mrs Rivers selected a heavy, velvet gown and as she hooked the bodice and settled the skirt, Anna wondered upon the necessity for a travelling dress. Some hours of tedium followed and once she had become used to the comfort and security derived from being dressed once more, Anna found the time heavy with dread and speculation. At last footsteps sounded in the corridor and as she caught her breath and half rose from her chair, the heavy lock was turned and the door opened.

Her visitor, as she knew it would be, was James. He stood for a moment framed in the doorway, and to her faint surprise he still seemed as handsome as ever; after her soul searching of the night she had half expected him to have lost his attractive appearance and to appear Satanically ugly.

"Go and find some nourishment in the kitchen," he told the woman by the fire briefly and she made haste to obey him.

Clutching the book she had been attempting to read, Anna eyed him coldly, trying to appear composed.

"Well, J-James," she said, her voice shaking a little, "do you intend to murder me first, or merely leave me here to die?"

Coming away from the door, he smiled thinly. "N-neither," he mocked. "At the moment, that is . . . I'll give no guarantee as to what will happen later."

Going across to her writing desk, he took out paper and quill, setting them on the sloping top. "Come here," he commanded quite pleasantly over his shoulder.

"Why?"

He sighed and turned back to her. "I wish you to write a letter," he said and forestalled her question by adding. "To your brother. Doubtless he'll realise your absence sometime, and an explanation from you that you have been ill and are now going with us to visit Ireland in order to convalesce will set his mind at rest."

"H-how thoughtful of you," commented the girl, "but, really, you know I'd rather Kit was worried."

"I am sure you would, but I find the thought of Kit raising a hue and cry far from attractive." For a moment he looked down at the seated girl, his thin brows drawn together in a black line. "You'll really be much wiser to obey me," he said, still pleasantly.

Something in his expression was immensely menacing and Anna shivered involuntarily as she met his blue gaze.

For a few more seconds she resisted, her breath quickening before reluctantly she gave in and seated herself at the elegant desk. Reflecting that she might be able to slip in a clue to her circumstances, she dipped her pen in the ink and waited for James' instructions.

"Write what I said," he commanded, "don't forget to mention that you have been ill."

"Why?" she asked, conversationally,

the quill scratching over the paper, spluttering ink with the nervous tremor of her hands.

"It — might be useful."

His words hung in the air and as their meaning sank in, she looked up quickly, finding his eyes so bleak and cold that she gasped and closed her own, shutting out the sight of his ruthless gaze.

"J-James," she appealed faintly.

The pen, that she had not realised she had dropped, was replaced firmly in her hand. "Write, Anna," commanded James, implacably and silently she obeyed him.

"I don't believe Cessy will stand by and see me come to harm," she said, bravely, as he sprinkled sand over the wet ink.

"My dear sister, has shown her true colours and persuaded that fool Weston to remove her to the safety of his mother's home. She crept out before dawn this morning — so don't look for help from that quarter."

Realising the meaning behind the Irish girl's note, Anna's heart sank at the thought of being quite alone with James and his aunt, who now suddenly assumed the appearance in her imagination of two ruthless monsters.

Folding and sealing her letter, James slipped it into his pocket. "Be ready to leave this afternoon," he said curtly, starting towards the door.

"My clothes — " ventured Anna, waiting breathlessly for his answer which would tell her a great deal.

"Leave them," he said carelessly. "Take only what you will need over night."

When she was alone, Anna sat very still, hugging herself. James' words had made it very plain that he considered the transporting of her belongings unnecessary which could lead her only to one supposition — a view which until then she had pushed firmly away each time it arose. Now she forced herself to face squarely the fact that the Jacobites considered her too dangerous to be allowed to live.

Shuddering, she bit her knuckles, forcing back the wild fear that threatened to overwhelm her. Resolutely she viewed the situation; knowing that she could never escape from the room or overcome

Mrs Rivers, the journey seemed the only chance that might afford her release and she decided that she must take the first opportunity that presented itself, regardless of the risk involved.

The hours dragged on. The house was inordinately quiet and she knew that the servants must have left. Mrs Rivers sat beside the dead fire, occasionally sipping discreetly from her gin bottle, but never so much as to incapacitate herself and watching the girl all the while. Anna jumped to her feet almost with eagerness and stood facing the door as James entered.

A voluminous travelling cloak swung out behind him, thrown back over his shoulders to reveal his plain burgundy coloured suit and serviceable sword he wore. Recognising the small phial he carried, Anna backed away, warding him off with both hands.

"No, James," she cried, remembering the effect of the drug previously and that she would need her wits about her if she was to escape. "Please don't make me drink that. I promise I won't make a scene."

She allowed her despair and disquiet to show and James eyed her consideringly, noting her distraught air. "Your word?" he asked at last.

Anna nodded eagerly, with no intention of keeping her pledge and her captor returned the phial to his pocket.

"And if you prove difficult, we can always use it later," he pointed out. Suddenly he swept her a bow and crooked his arm invitingly. "Come, Anna, the coach is waiting." Smiling with a hint of his old charm, he tucked her hand into his elbow. "You've lost, my dear, admit it with good grace and let us be friends again . . . at least for the journey."

Anna fought the revulsion his touch brought and forced her hand to lay passive within his grasp. "I've been so unhappy," she whispered, hanging her head and allowing a small sob to escape.

Patting her shoulder soothingly with his free hand, "I admit that I've been a little unkind and said some things which I didn't mean," he said, "but I am afraid you deserved to be punished. Now dry your eyes, be good and we'll say no more about it."

To her satisfaction Anna saw that he accepted her play-acting and continuing in her role of simple, lovelorn womanhood, allowed him to fasten her travelling cloak about her shoulders.

As she left the house on James' arm one glance told her that Ben occupied the doorway opposite, his interest ostensibly elsewhere as she entered the coach and she suddenly realized how much she had been counting on his seeing her departure and reporting to Rafe Bellamy.

A picture of the red-haired soldier rose before her eyes and it was as much as she could do not to snatch her hand away from her companion as he helped her into the coach.

Lady Primrose was already comfortably ensconced in the luxurious interior but, preoccupied with her own thoughts, Anna hardly noticed her presence. With sudden, astounding clarity she had been brought face to face with her own deepest emotions and suddenly forced to admit to feelings which she had hidden even from herself.

Sinking back in her corner, and

closing her eyes as the word was given and the horses started forward, she deliberately probed deeper with a feeling half pleasure, half pain admitting at last, that the feeling she had been nourishing toward Captain Bellamy all this time, while akin to hate was in fact very far from it.

One bitter-sweet tear escaped and trickled down her cheek; now that it was too late she knew with the utmost certainly that she loved the man who had been the means of inveigling her into the business of spying and thinking back she was almost sure that he had returned her affections at one time. Cursing her foolishness and regretting her championship of the unworthy James, she opened her eyes and found Lady Primrose regarding her closely.

The older woman smiled and offered Anna a book from the pile on the seat beside her. "Do have something to read. I always find travelling so tedious, myself."

Accepting the book, Anna viewed her companion curiously, wondering if the older woman intended to treat her as if nothing untoward had happened during the last few days. Lady Primrose's next words confirmed her surmise.

"You'll like Ireland, I'm sure. After London it will prove a little quiet, no doubt, but I'm sure you'll not be sorry for a few restful days."

"After being drugged and abducted, you mean," said Anna, finding herself not prepared to go along with the other's pretence.

"We live in rather a remote spot," went on Lady Primrose, as if she had not spoken. "With very few neighbours, but you'll find that we make our own amusements."

"Just you and I?" asked Anna truculently. "James, no doubt, will be away arranging a wild rebellion somewhere and Cessy, I understand has other arrangements."

"The dear child is betrothed," smiled the older woman. "She and Mr Weston have known each other for an age, as you know and when she made her feelings known to me, I gave my consent at once."

"I thought she ran off," observed Anna, gazing out of the window at the passing city.

"My dear, Anna," Lady Primrose said cuttingly, "if you are intent upon being provoking I shall turn my attention elsewhere." Flipping open a book, she flicked over a few pages and ostentatiously gave the closely printed page all her interest.

The clock in the hall had been allowed to run down and Anna had missed his strident telling of the hours. Consequently she had no way of telling the time, but realised that it must have been considerably past noon when they left Essex Street, for the sun was well past its zenith and already the late afternoon shadows were lengthening. Glancing out of the window, she could see James riding alongside the coach, with two out-riders further back.

"Do we stop the night at an Inn?" she inquired hopefully.

Lady Primrose's eyebrows rose as she replied without lifting her glance from her book. "My dear, Anna, how naïve," she said, abandoning pretence for a moment.

"We'll stay with friends of course — *our* friends."

She allowed time for her meaning to sink in before returning to her reading, but appeared unable to relax for some reason, her eyes wandering to the window every few minutes.

"It's growing dusk already," remarked Anna, watching her companion and knew she had struck the right reason behind the other's agitation when Lady Primrose raised anxious eyes.

"We were later starting than I intended," she said absently. "I only hope we are across Hampstead Heath before dark."

"Hampstead Heath! I supposed we would take the Edgware Road — surely we are going to Holyhead?"

Lady Primrose glanced at her impatiently. "So we are — but tonight we'll stay with friends who happen to live on the other side of the Heath."

Despair filled Anna as she realised that Captain Bellamy, supposing the coach on its way to Anglesea where they could take ship for Ireland, would have no idea as to her whereabouts. Accepting how much she had been banking on the soldier coming to her rescue, she stared out of the window, reviewing the situation and sudden anger began to replace her dejection.

"I hope there's a whole hoard of highwaymen waiting for us," she said viciously, kicking her heel against the secret trapdoor in the floor. "I shall *enjoy* telling them where you hide your valuables!"

But as it happened, when the coach was brought to a sudden and unexpected stop sometime later on the most wild and desolate part of the heath, Anna seized the moment of confusion to wrench open the far door and slip out into the night, taking refuge in a convenient clump of bushes.

Drawing her cloak closer about her, she peered out, taking in the scene before her; a horseman on either side of the road sat their mounts immovably, the pale moonlight glinting on the dull metal of the pistols they were pointing at the coach and its escort.

"I want the girl," said one of the highwaymen, to Anna's amazement and even as her mind whirled in sudden supposition, she noticed that the man nearest her, while he sat his horse in a military manner, carried his arm stiffly. Eyes wide she studied the other man; surely there was something decidedly familiar about his bearing. Common sense told her that no ordinary Tobyman could possibly know of her, or any other girl's presence in the coach and she almost started forward, before a new thought struck her. Could this be the means James and his cahoots had devised for her removal, she wondered as an icy shiver ran down her spine and her knees weakened.

Biting her lip with indecision she hesitated almost crying with frustration. Suddenly the man on the far side of the road, urged his horse forward, bending low over the animal's neck to peer into the coach.

"Anna!" he called. "Come out."

Her heart leaping with gladness as she recognised the familiar voice, she gathered up her skirts and darted forward realising her mistake only as all eyes were involuntarily turned on her as she called out. Seizing the diversion she had created, James snatched a pistol from his saddle-holster and fired it at the man by the coach horses, flinging himself almost in the same moment at Rafe Bellamy.

As the two men rolled on the ground, Lady Primrose screeched at the coachman and obeying her command the man whipped up his horses and the clumsy coach started forward. Taking their opportunity the two out-riders made off in the opposite direction, leaving Anna and the other mounted man alone with the two men struggling silently on the damp earth.

With its usual perversity the moon had hidden behind thick clouds and in the darkness the adversaries were indistinguishable. Suddenly they broke apart, one leaped to his feet and drew his sword, wrenching at the fastening of his cloak and the other climbed to his feet.

"Just you and I, Mr Drelincourt," said Rafe, a little breathlessly, raising the point of his weapon.

"I had not supposed you so melo-dramatic," remarked James.

The other's eyes slid away to where Anna stood. "This is personal," he said, his voice clear and deadly.

"I — see," said James, following his gaze. "The winner takes the girl — "

"No — you've forgotten Mr Weston, Anna goes free whatever happens."

James looked towards the other man who stood silently beside his horse and shrugged. "As you will," he said, contemptuously and tossing back his cloak, drew his own sword.

As the metal slithered free, the soft, deadly sound filled Anna with dread and taking a quick breath she ran forward.

"No, oh no," she cried. "Rafe, please don't — !"

Her arm was taken from behind and Jason Weston held her firmly, while the two men saluted briefly before warily circling each other, like two curs seeking for an opening. Watching, Anna saw James leap forward, and closed her eyes in horror as the sound of clashing steel and muffled tramp of heavy boots filled the silent night. The clouds rolled away and moonlight played across the scene, lighting it like a play, draining all colour but striking contrast from the men's suits and lace ruffles.

Lunging and parrying the men appeared to be taking part in some beautiful but lethal dance, only their laboured breathing betraying the effort each was making. The end came quite suddenly — James lunged forward, his body, arm and sword in one deadly line, pointing straight towards Rafe's heart as he ventured all on the one effort. Receiving the attack, the soldier parried James' thrust and the point of the other's sword slid past his chest. At full stretch James was off balance and before he could recover Rafe took the opportunity and plunged forward his sword posed precisely as he spitted his opponent neatly above the elbow.

"Enough?" he panted, standing back, his sword held lightly, but ready to return to the 'enguard' position if necessary.

James' weapon had fallen from his nerveless fingers as he clasped his other hand tightly about his arm. Already blood was seeping between his fingers and he swayed slightly as he breathed heavily. "I surrender," he said thickly.

"My dear fellow, you'd be more of an encumbrance than anything else. Neither

I nor my employers have any desire for another Jacobite martyr," Rafe told him, cuttingly as he pulled his cravat from his neck and twisted it about the other's arm. "Mount your horse and go — and if you take my advice you'll not return for a good while. I'm afraid you'll find that London will be bad for your health until this matter is forgotten."

Wordlessly James turned away and stumbled to his waiting horse, dragging himself into the saddle. Gathering the reins into his good hand he stared down at the watching group, his gaze so full of brooding threat and menace that Anna gasped and shrank back, as he rode away.

"Well, Anna?" Rafe asked as the hoof beats died away, stretching his hand towards her a little uncertainly.

"R-Rafe," she whispered, her eyes searching his face. Suddenly she was in his arms, held tight against his chest as she trembled with relief and clutched at him with desperate fingers. "I — thought you'd be killed," she cried.

"Would you have cared?" he asked and gathered her closer as he read the answer on her raised face. Rocking her gently, he rested his cheek against her hair.

"Thank Heaven for Ben," said Anna.

"And Cecilia."

"Cessy!" Anna looked up.

"How else do you think I knew where they were taking you? She used her ears before leaving Essex Street."

"But — how did she know?"

"Miss Drelincourt seems to have more brains than we credited her with. She'd noticed Ben and when she suspected you were a prisoner, sought him out."

Anna turned her head towards Ensign Weston. "James said she was with your mother?" she asked uncertainly.

Jason nodded. "She'd never been a fervent Jacobite and as her affection for me grew so her interest in the Stuart cause waned. It needed only your plight to set her resolve . . . she effected her escape from Lady Primrose's house very neatly."

Anna smiled at the admiration in his voice and offered him her congratulations. "I hope you'll both be very happy," she said.

"No doubt of it," he answered simply,

swinging himself into his saddle and preparing to ride off. "You have no need of my escort, for we'll have frightened off every self-respecting Tobyman within miles," he pointed out, "and Cessy will be waiting for news." His eyes went to Rafe. "What shall I tell her?" he asked.

"Say that her brother is taking a tour of the Continent and Lady Primrose had returned 'poste-haste' to Ireland. She need not vex herself about repercussions — Whitehall is as anxious to cover the matter as the Stuart factor . . . We took care not to catch the Prince."

As Jason Weston tipped his tricorn with his riding-crop and rode away, Anna looked up at Captain Bellamy. "Did you mean that? About not catching the Prince?"

Leading her towards his patiently waiting horse, the soldier nodded. "Of course — we'd leifer far that he was safe in Paris than languishing in some English jail, a rallying point for all the wild, romantic adventurers waiting to give their life to some lost cause."

"Is that what it is?" she asked, her eyes wide.

Lifting her up onto his horse's neck, he mounted behind her, one arm holding her firmly as he urged the animal forward.

"It is now," he told her quietly, as the horse's hooves clopped softly over the damp earth. "I'll wager he ventured all on this last throw. His followers might try to recoup their losses, but I think Charles Edward's heart won't be in it."

"I'm — almost sorry," murmured Anna, her mind on the Prince as she had last seen him.

"He's not the stuff Kings are made of," Rafe said matter of factly. "In a few years he'll be a melancholy, old drunkard."

Anna flinched from his forthright view. "It might have been different — " she ventured.

"And if it had — we might not have met," the Captain reminded her.

Turning her head, Anna studied his face, her eyes soft as she met his grey gaze. "Then, poor Prince — I'm glad," she whispered, her breath caressing his cheek.

His arm tightened as if he would never let her go. "Anna — my love," he said and bending forward found her mouth, as the horse, indifferent to the two riders it carried jogged on along the white ribbon of moonlit road towards the distant lights of an Inn.

Secure in the circle of his arm, Anna leaned back against Rafe's shoulder. Sleepily, she watched the nearing lights, content to let her future lie in the hands of the man who carried her, certain in the knowledge that she had found her own true love sometime during the Prince's disastrous summer. Sighing for him, she nestled closer, forgetting all save her love — as she and Rafe rode away from the dangers that had beset them towards whatever the future might hold.

THE END

Other titles in the
Ulverscroft Large Print Series:

TO FIGHT THE WILD
Rod Ansell and Rachel Percy

Lost in uncharted Australian bush, Rod Ansell survived by hunting and trapping wild animals, improvising shelter and using all the bushman's skills he knew.

COROMANDEL
Pat Barr

India in the 1830s is a hot, uncomfortable place, where the East India Company still rules. Amelia and her new husband find themselves caught up in the animosities which seethe between the old order and the new.

THE SMALL PARTY
Lillian Beckwith

A frightening journey to safety begins for Ruth and her small party as their island is caught up in the dangers of armed insurrection.